Other titles by Patrick Summers

Key Change:
An Alternative History of Mozart

A Collection of Brevities

The Prison of Time: Poems from 2023

The Spirit of This Place:
How Music Illuminates the Human Spirit

BIRDIE'S
FOREVER DAY

A Novel by
Patrick Summers

Contenti Press

ISBN 979-8-9926151-1-1

Cover and book design by Pattima Singhalaka.

Dedication

This a work of fiction, though Birdie was a real person, my aunt, married to my dad's brother, and I dedicate this book to her memory.

What I have attempted here is not a biography. All of the characters besides Birdie are amalgams, and I've morphed them together just as she often did. Similarly, the events described are both true and delusional, told with whole sentences she often uttered. She was not a liar; everything she said was absolutely true to her, whether or not it was true to others, while liars knowingly spin truths into lies. Birdie, though, pieced together fragmented memories in an unusually poetic and childish way. She often lived in fantasies; she wallowed in years of grief, yet she was also joyous. I've tried to echo her cadence and grammar, which cared nothing for subject–verb agreement, and sounded somewhere between homespun country-talk and the mid-Atlantic tones of Hollywood's golden era. This book has brought me the joy of remembering her, and I felt a deep need to commit her to paper, however imperfectly, for who will remember her if I do not? I actually do not know how many of her recollections were true, so in this rendering of her I invite you into what I felt as an admiring little boy who loved her: imagination is an endlessly renewing world of forever days.

Patrick Summers

All our religions founder, you
remain, small sunburnt *deus loci*
safe in your natal shrine,
landscape of the precocious southern heart,
continuously revived in passion's common
tragic and yet incorrigible spring:
in every special laughter overheard,
your specimen is everything—
accents of the little cackling god,
part animal, part insect, and part bird.

From "Deus Loci," Lawrence Durrell

CHAPTER 1

B y now I know that names have magic inside them, if only because
my own name has proved itself to me. Mama never told me why she
named me Birdie, but I was perfectly named.

Slick wasn't. His really was a nickname that left him not quite knowing
himself. He came from one of them big Catholic families that was spread
like ants all over southern Indiana, and his grandparents was mostly
direct Irish. Most of the folks here in Ophelia were Irish. Not far from
here, though, in Jasper, all the families was German and I even remember
hearing them *talk* in German until the first war. Lands, our little Baptist
brood was less than half the size of Slick's family. His little brothers and
sisters couldn't say his born name, Clayton, so it came out as Slick. He's
the only man I ever met named Clayton, and I thought it was such a
beautiful name. Truth be told, I took more of a shining to his name at
first than I did to him. I tried like crazy to get people to call him Clayton
after we got married, but the childhood habits stick close in little towns
like ours. His grandma told me once that he'd been named after a village
in England where they lived before they came to Indiana, back before the
Civil War. I knew about that almost my whole life, but I didn't remember
it until I got here. Isn't that strange?

Most people forget things when they get older but I never was like
most people. I couldn't forget things! I only ever had one *real* forever day,
and until it happened, you never could have told me that I hadn't already
had a whole lot more of them. My forever day was the last day I was really

happy, before the reckoning. We've all known them people, the ones who spend their whole lives in one or two stories, instead of the people who are always looking for a new one. The lookers, I always wonder what their forever days are like. They sure can't be like mine.

After he retired from doctoring, Doc Chattin had a whole new life making us paintings out of string and I loved them so much. They was just string on top of felt but they were beautiful. He spent all of his time making them for everybody and his wife made him give them away because he made so many. He gave us birds, of course, a beautiful big owl that I hung up over the old pump organ I got when they closed the old Methodist Church in Ophelia. It had Jesus and Mary carved into it, but I loved that it also had little birds.

I'm getting used to wherever this is, the place I'm in now. There is nothing here that belongs to anybody else. What was always mine still is, all of my words and my thoughts. You can't think about thoughts, can you? They just are. But here you have to at least think a little bit about yourself and what you think about, because you have to make sense of it. All those things Mama used to say that I didn't really hear at the time, yet I still remember them. They mean more to me now. She used to sit in Ophelia and read the Bible out loud: "There were fourteen generations in all from Abraham to David, fourteen from David to the exile to Babylon, and fourteen from the exile to the Messiah," from the book of Matthew 1:17. I still remember it. And I've figured out that my forever days, the ones I thought I had, came every fourteen years. I've just learned that, but Mama knew it from way back. Over here, you don't *know* everything. You don't even know everything you yourself once knew. But somehow everything is clearer.

People here know so much. I mean, they did over there, too, but I didn't know *them*, and now I think I do. Over there, so much has happened in the past that you can't make hide nor hair of it, at least I couldn't. Somebody asked me if I missed my little hometown of Ophelia, and of course I do in my way, but I am also never leaving it. How could I? My whole time there I had no idea that Ophelia was named for a lady character by Shakespeare, a lady who drowned. I mean, why didn't Mama or somebody ever tell me that? During the first war, we had all them pageants and things, both in Ophelia and at The Ritz over in Loogootee, and a couple of times we even had real Shakespeare actors come through. I never understood them, but I sure did love seeing them. You'd think somebody would have said something. I don't know if it would have made a difference, but those things are nice to know, aren't they?

I remember wanting to be in the Indian pageant at The Ritz in the worst way. I begged Mama for weeks and weeks to let me be in the show, and she was not happy with the idea at all because she didn't know what kind of people was putting it on. So many of the vaudevillians that came through southern Indiana in those years were charlatans and womanizers.

Mama let me do it in the end, I guess because of the way I saved money to buy all of the decorations for my Injun costume. Every detail of the costume was important to me. I had collected bird feathers for days, all around the town, and I knew where to find them, too: on the ground at the feet of buildings on Main Street, where birds perched through the spring and summer. I always found great feathers around the Dime Store, because it had all those little crevices and statues carved into the top of the building, which was the tallest thing in town besides the church steeples until they put up that awful water tower.

Mama remembered the Dime Store building being built in 1890, and it was so important to the ones who built the store that they carved the year into a block on the side. And there was carved birds in permanent flight away from that "1890" stone, all over the building, as though they was being set free from something. Through my whole life I never got tired of picking up feathers there or looking at the carvings. They had fourteen birds carved in that building, and I knew every one of them, even had names for each one when I was growing up. Of course, in the 1970s they took that whole front of the building away, saying the stone birds weren't safe and they might fall on somebody. Everything good got taken away.

CHAPTER 2

My little hometown, Ophelia, was such a wonderful forever place, quiet and sweet most of the time. I know I will never leave it. It was just downriver of a shoal in the misnamed White River, which was never anything other than a muddy light brown, but that never kept us kids from getting in that river and swimming like Huck Finn. I liked better the little creeks that fed into it, especially Lost River, because in the feeder streams you could see all the way to the bottom—no mud, no distractions, and if there was snakes you could see them.

Usually we went swimming out to Hindostan Falls, where there was a little area downriver of the falls but protected by a huge flat rock where you could still see the outlines of the buildings that used to be there. Mama knew some people who had lived in Hindostan but a plague came, something like cholera, and killed almost all of them, and the ones that could fled to Ophelia or Loogootee to start over. The river was everything to us, and we shared its moods. The west side of the river was hilly and beautiful, where I lived as a girl and then in another house where Slick and I lived right up until I came here. The east side, where the main street was, and the churches and the high school, was more flat, and so more liable to flood, and the world of Ophelia went crazy in 1913, when I was just coming to girlhood, and that river flooded beyond anything anyone alive could remember, and I was reared with people with parents who remembered the Civil War. Everybody kept saying the flood was "biblical," and I still go all chicken flesh when I think about the water coming up into our little valley below McCormick Street. Biblical.

I was brought up on the Bible, and I did try in my way to live my life by it, but I didn't go in for all them Bible-people around town who tried to always turn you to their way of thinking. Mama was the best person I ever knew, but it wasn't because she went to church or because she read her Bible every day. She did that because that is what everybody did. Like anybody who knew her, I admired her because of what she *did* in her life, the way she spoke to people, the way she was so kind all the time. I tried like everything to ape the way she lived. She didn't have the bad thoughts about people that I had, but I couldn't help having them. Working in the telephone office, I heard every single thing that went on in Ophelia for years and in the surrounding towns, too. There was people who would ring through and I couldn't even listen to their conversations because there was so much hatred and fear in their voices. That was rare, though. I *always* listened in, but I was not a gossip, so nobody ever knew about it.

You see, almost all of Ophelia except the two doctors had party lines, so there weren't much of a way for people to have secrets. Now, if you *were* on a party line and you picked up the phone while people was talking, there was a little beep that let people know you had joined the call. The only way around that was if you picked up the phone at *exactly* the same time I put it through, then the person you were listening in on didn't know, but I did. I could see that the line was open, so I knew exactly who was listening in and who was gossiping. I would hear rumors about people, and I always knew exactly who spread them.

Most of our telephone calls were local. Ophelia was so small we didn't even have call letters, just a few numbers. Older folks had four, younger ones five, and I never had to look at a telephone book. I could listen in on the calls that went to farther places like Indianapolis or Louisville. I heard about the affairs, the family fights, all about everybody's last wills, and the final truths of their diseases. I always knew who was going to die before everybody else, as the emergency calls came to me first.

There was nothing that got by me in those days, though none of my forever days happened at the telephone office. I liked knowing so much and saying nothing about any of it.

I heard prayers, too, all the time, in calls to preachers and midwives. I heard pain in voices when a loved one was getting ready to pass over. But I also heard them lying and calculating and making excuses for bills they didn't pay and people they hurt and wives they cheated on. I heard them call the liquor stores to see if they had a shipment that day, because they had guzzled down every drop of whiskey they'd bought the week before. People in Ophelia were always mindful of what people thought of them, so they would buy a certain amount of liquor here before they'd drive to other towns to buy the rest, thinking no one would notice they was a drunk. I could see it from my perch at the phone office. I heard the ones who intentionally hurt others, and they was the ones I couldn't stand and I would always find ways to be sure they somehow paid a price for what they did, even if it just meant creating a suspicion in them that *somebody* might know. And they would curse on the phone. I hate all cursing, but especially all them church sitters in Ophelia who would pretend to be so holy on Sundays then thought nothing of cursing every other day. Didn't God hear all of those things that I was also hearing when I listened on the phone lines? But God could actually do something about their problems if He wanted to. All I could do was notice what hypocrites they all were. I sure couldn't go sit in a church every Sunday with them, knowing what I knew. For a few years in my little Indiana town, in my own quiet way, I had the power of a God, yet I chose to never use it. I've never, ever, told anyone anything I learned.

CHAPTER 3

It was when I worked at the phone office that I learned how to divine things through the phone lines, at least the surfaces of feelings and dangers, but a lot of words was hard for me to remember, even if the caller spoke clear. It used to drive them crazy that they would give me the exchange or some other instruction and I would forget it, but I simply could not remember things like that. Numbers were fine, but words confused me. I kept a notepad at my desk to write down all the words. When I would read the words out at the end of my shift, I nearly always knew exactly what they meant, but at the moment I needed them they would fail me, so then I'd feel awful guilty. It was like that my whole life: when I really needed to remember things, I just couldn't.

Nobody pays any mind to people like me. I was working in the phone office on that awful Thursday before the more-awful Friday. Thursday morning I looked out the window of the office, and I'd never seen so many birds in one place in my life. Mostly they was blackbirds, but I saw a few sparrows and finches—and what scared the dickens out of me was that two mourning doves were perched on the window ledge right outside the window by my desk. I hadn't seen a pair of those so close up since I was a little girl. Mama would never let Daddy kill doves because they mate for life, and she said it wasn't right to kill an animal that devoted itself to another creature, as that would fly in the face of God. "We must always encourage the mating of two creatures. That reminds us of the creation." I always remember the things Mama said.

Well, those two mourning doves on the ledge and all those birds outside crowded onto every single telephone line within sight, and made me nervous. Ophelia was one of the few places that still had phone operators in 1963, and I like to think they kept the two of us on, me and Madge, because they liked us. Mr. Arvin, who owned the exchange, was such a kindly man. Madge and I both knew that the minute he passed on, the phones in Ophelia would convert over to the modern phones everybody else had. There was no stopping that progress, but Mr. Arvin liked the old ways. He even stuck to having an outhouse on his beautiful old house south of town, long after he had an indoor privy installed before the war! He'd seen a lot in his life, since he'd been born just after the Civil War, so we had to always be on call for the news that his life was over, but darned if he didn't make it past a century, living almost until my forever day in 1973. Can you imagine? He liked the old ways and I loved that about him. He was such a good man, the kind you don't see anymore. Men who lived that long and saw all the darkness growing in the world, whether they knew it or not, were the truly great people.

I called Mr. Arvin that day and told him about the mourning doves on the ledge. He asked me if I knew what they were trying to say. I told him I didn't rightly know, but there was a lot of birds gathered on every phone line, thousands of them, and whenever that happened I was always afraid of one of them wild boys coming into town and starting to shoot at them.

"Lord, Birdie, I can hear it in your voice: you're so nervous right now you couldn't piss in a river. Cool yourself down, now."

He always talked that way. Not quite cursing but not quite comfortable, neither. He always kept things on the edge of what he knew was fitting, like most men I ever met in my life. But he was right on that Thursday. I *was* terribly nervous, because I knew the birds were gathering that morning for a reason. They were listening to what was going through the phone lines. I saw it in my own way several times that day and all the next morning. I saw an energy, and on that day I finally believed there was something like a devil. With the war, I'd seen that energy, too, but those forces on that day were beyond even the birds. This energy, on that chilly

Thursday, was so vicious, so unexpected, and these men meant business. The birds were trying to tell me that these men meant business. I plugged into every phone line I had, trying to hear them, but all I could do was see the effects of what they were talking about, see that the birds were upset. On that Thursday morning they was more than upset—they were panicked. They would swoop up into great circles over the Pinnacle, over to the park, and back to the phone lines by my office, over and over. I could see what was happening: they were hearing terrible news over the phone lines, spending their energy about the danger for a few minutes of flight, and then coming back to listen to more.

I worked the early shift that Friday so I could get home to watch my soaps. Around 11:30, when I got home, all the bird feeders were empty, so I slowly filled them back up. When I finally sat down, I noticed the house was darker than it should be at that time of day. I remember it because I was home in time for *As the World Turns* at 2:00, just like always. I went back to the front porch and the entire house was covered in birds. I was petrified. I couldn't open a window or door, there were so many of them. I hadn't seen anything like it in my whole life, not even the day that the Japs bombed Pearl Harbor when the birds had acted so strangely. This was definitely something else again. So, the birds had me penned into the house. I called Slick and explained it to him. He said they would all fly away when he pulled in the driveway, and if they didn't, he would go outside and make a lot of noise and scare them off. That made me feel a little safer. I knew they couldn't get into the house, but I was still so scared.

I'd heard that year about an awful new movie, *The Birds*, but I couldn't bear to go see a movie that made birds look so scary and sexual. But I sure thought about it that day when they surrounded my house. Were they trying to tell me something? Our dog Ginger was so happy I was home that day. She got up on the couch with me and fell asleep. She seemed not to notice the birds at all, so I was happy for that. We must have both drifted off to sleep, because I lost all track of whatever program was on. I was having a dream about a big car surrounded by tall buildings when suddenly the birds all went flying in fear. There was a gunshot. It was close. I woke with such a start that I know I screamed out. Somebody in a car was going to be shot. The birds had told me, because they knew it was coming.

So, I was stunned on the very next day when I was finishing up work and the calls started coming in about President Kennedy being shot in Dallas. We always had a television going in the phone office, which you could half watch if you wanted to. Our callers couldn't hear it because we kept it low, but it did let me keep up on my soaps. That day *As the World Turns* was on and I always loved that show so much. But as soon as I heard what happened in Dallas, I could not stop sobbing. I'd known the death was coming, but I didn't know *enough* to stop it. Did anybody ever have a more useless power? I could see what was happening out of the free will of evil men, but I couldn't do a thing to stop it. All that Friday the exchange was lit up like a Christmas tree, and sometimes people were just calling in to share their grief with me, just so they wouldn't be alone in remembering the darkest day any of us would ever remember. When you work in a phone office on a day like that, when a President is shot, you don't have time to have feelings about it or to absorb what has happened. You are too busy. There isn't a moment to spare on those days. The tragedy only hits you later. Pearl Harbor was awful, but it was also distant and didn't feel so close to home. President Kennedy was loved around Ophelia just because he was Catholic, which made me not take a shine to him at all, but I was heartsore when he got killed. That poor Jackie, so beautiful, had to see all of that at her young age. I hate that awful Dallas, Texas—they killed our President. I know it wasn't the whole town, but I can't help how I feel. That is just a hateful place and I sure know I won't ever go there.

I left work when Madge got there around 11:00, crying like I'd never seen her cry before, and she was a crier. It hadn't hit me yet when I walked down the stairs to the main street. Across the street was Home Outfitters, where I knew there was a whole line of color televisions that would be on. I stood there for a long time watching the news and none of it was any good. President Kennedy was dead. Somebody got to him. But I knew they were all on the phone the day before, and I knew the birds were hearing it. I'll bet the birds all over the country were perched on phone lines listening to what was happening, but we don't have any way to hear what they heard.

CHAPTER 4

Slick's brothers all went to their outfit reunions after the second war, but Slick never once wanted to see anyone he met during the war. He seemed happy as pie to have that part of his life behind him forever. Even though he didn't see combat, he saw and heard about a lot of horror, and he was always such a sensitive man. He never talked about any part of the war to me or to anyone. He came home after being away for three years, got on with his life, and never brought it up. The only person from Camp McCoy he ever talked about was a priest who saw action in Europe and brought Slick back a real Bavarian cuckoo clock. We still have it right in our dining room. It was from the old Germany, the one before the war and before Hitler, so I let it stay. The priest came back to St. Meinrad and I think he was there for years. I loved that cuckoo clock, and I can still hear it clear as a bell in my memory. I hope Jenny took care of that clock so that some other greedy members of the family didn't get it. All the nieces and nephews wanted it.

CHAPTER 5

I've said it many times since I got here, though I'm not sure yet who I'm talking to: I've been in my forever day now for a while. It was spring of 1973, I think. Oh, how I loved those early '70s years, before the unraveling. Little Jenny was about ten. Stevie was sixteen. My favorite niece and favorite nephew were still so cute. He was my great-nephew, actually, though they was sure from two very different parts of the family. I paid more attention to Stevie because his so-called mother was such a lowlife. I never did like her and still can't believe my idiot nephew would marry such a goofus. She was the one, not me, who should never have been allowed to have children, and I don't mind saying so. Gerry, Stevie's mom, had a very strong personality, which is a nice way of saying she is rude and loud to everyone. She was one of several people I avoided because she was so willful that she made you act like her. After I'd been around her a bit I, noticed I started putting sentences together like she did, without the cursing, of course, and using some of her words. I think it must take a demon to make you change the way you speak. I couldn't avoid her nearly as much I wanted to because Stevie kept coming to me for help and advice. He needed a mother and she just wasn't one. Oh, that woman pert near ruined my life.

That winter of '73, though, Jenny was still in her innocence, and Stevie hadn't yet permanently moved into all his darkness. For Christmas of '72, I'd found some electronic recording equipment for him and he absolutely loved it, was over all the time fiddling with it, first in our basement and finally I made him move it all to the garage to get that noise out of the house. That fool mother of his wouldn't even let him take the stuff home. She said they "didn't have room," when she sure enough found room for all of the useless junk she wanted, and plenty of room for her Scotch bottles. I spent more on Stevie than on any of the others, but dang it, Stevie had more of an uphill climb than most.

Jenny wanted the same thing that she'd wanted since she was three years old: piano sheet music and history books about music, so I found her some that she seemed to like. I had a ton of sheet music because I bought every song sheet out there, and she played through those nice enough, but they weren't where her heart was. She wanted books on opera, can you imagine?

I found the ones she wanted in Bloomington, where there was a lot of music around. That girl could play anything on the piano right from the very start, and she was quite a sight with her little legs not able to reach the pedals yet that winter, so I glued an old shoe onto a block of wood so she could reach the right pedal on the piano. She would start at one end of the hymnal and play for hours through dozens and dozens of them. Some of them I hadn't heard since I was a little girl: "Work, for the night is coming, work through the morning hours; work while the dew is sparkling, work 'mid springing flowers." Hymns from my childhood would make my soul change color, as sure as the summer leaves change. No music was more beautiful to me. I'm not proud that I never went to church after childhood, but the old hymns still fill me with a kind of joy that nothing else in life ever did. I always thought that if I saw the Grand Canyon or the Eiffel Tower I might feel it, too; but since I never saw those things and knew I never would, I more than contented myself with the hymns.

That winter we got a huge snow, and Jenny was with us for four days because her parents was snowed in with the cousins up in Indianapolis. The house was filled with music when Jenny was around. Slick was still working and still had all his mind. I didn't think it was possible to be sentimental about a gas station, but Slick's station was finally beautiful by the time of my forever day in 1973. He had the outside covered in white steel the summer before, covering up all that awful white cinder block, and he did the trimming in blue and yellow that matched the big Sunoco sign at the road. It was a little showplace that winter, and in the heavy snow it looked like something out of *The Wizard of Oz*. I liked that it looked like a White Castle restaurant, where they made my very favorite hamburger in the whole world, out of many choices! They only had White Castles in the big cities, so when we would go to Indianapolis or Louisville, Slick and I would buy twenty-five of those little hamburgers and eat them right then and there, then buy another seventy-five to take home and freeze. People thought we was crazy, but I could have lived on them White Castle burgers. The White Steamer in Washington was a family-owned place but they dressed up their little corner store to look like the White Castles, and even when other restaurants would come and go, there they sat, still in business. It wasn't as nice but we sure went there a lot, whenever we couldn't get away to the big cities. The White Steamer was the best restaurant around, if you didn't count fancy places like Hillie's or Marone's that put tablecloths on. Those places were not for me.

CHAPTER 6

You can't realize it until you are somewhere truly quiet, but the world is in every way too noisy. I know the noise bothered the birds but it didn't bother me as much as it should. It wasn't just all the surface noises we have now, with all the cars and trucks and lawn mowers, but people talk much more and much louder than they ever used to. I know that from the phones. When I was a girl, the only noise everybody shared was the trains. In winter, with no leaves to muffle them, we could hear their deep rumblings for a long time before they arrived. I loved hearing them echo around the hills. If I happened to be playing near the Pinnacle or the Jug Rock, or even miles away out at Hindostan, I could hear them and they always seemed to be coming from different directions. It was the quiet of the dense woods that drew me, even when I was a little girl, to get away from the plague of noise. I used to love the sound of the trains. Then, all of a sudden, I couldn't stand to ever hear them, because every time they would rumble in the distance, all I could remember was Daddy. I'll talk about him later.

But even though they was noisy, I miss going to the county fairs and seeing everybody's exhibits, all the wonderful pies and cakes, and seeing the things people spend their time on. I didn't care about the rides. They seemed to get wilder every year. And sometimes they would have haunted houses; I never liked them. But there was such joy in other parts of the fairs, in the beauty pageants and the food. Oh, to taste one of them corn dogs again! I could just live on them corn dogs. I stopped going to our local fair years ago because they actually gave a whole concert of gypsy music. I cannot for the life of me figure out why anyone would want to go to a whole night of gypsy music, and I sure would not give my money to a fair that would invite a bunch of gypsies and try to say they were good people. Those gypsies near ruined my whole life, and there some of them were up on stage!

I used to go to the area churches on Saturday afternoons to clean up the rice they threw after weddings, because that rice upset birds' stomachs. I wrote letters to every church for years trying to get them to throw birdseed instead, and finally—finally—after years of trying, the Catholics switched to birdseed. It always has to start with the Catholics. Once the biggest church in town did that, so did all of the others. Though it took a while, I consider it one of the victories of my life, because it kept rice out of the bellies of a lot of birds. I could tell the birds was happier about it, because after all the summer weddings, all those warm Saturday afternoons, you could hear the joy in their songs.

CHAPTER 7

It was a full scandal when Slick and I got married at the Baptist church, because in 1928 you simply did not marry outside the faith of your raising. Like most people in southern Indiana, Slick was Catholic, so we were considered a mixed marriage even though we were both as white as Sunday linens. He was also younger than I was and that wasn't done in those days, either, but I was twenty-eight and people would talk about you in those days if you waited that long to marry. Girls married their own age and their own church, so I broke both of those rules right quick. I didn't care. I knew he was the one I wanted to be with. I first knew about him after the big social that celebrated the end of the first war, though it was almost ten more years before we married, can you imagine? Even though he was still so young then, I could tell he had a sweetness about him, and the light around him was softer than on others. The birds liked him, too, and that was important to me. Every time he came around, the groundlings would gather to look at him, like the pictures you see of the soldiers watching Churchill or Eisenhower.

Our wedding was very small, just Mama and one of Slick's brothers, plus the nun, of course. Well, she wasn't a nun quite then but she had started to be one. The nun was Slick's youngest sister and she insisted on being there even though it was in the county courthouse and not in the church, which she did not like at all but she didn't say anything, at least not then. She was allowed to disapprove of our wedding, but naturally, I wasn't supposed to say a word about how young she was being swept up in the church like that.

The nun was around for everything in our lives, even though she taught up north and spent her summers at St. Mary-of-the-Woods up in Terre Haute. Whenever she came to visit, she stayed with us because we were the one couple in her family that didn't have kids, and she didn't want her other brothers or sisters to feel "put out." She sure didn't mind putting me out. Oh, she was very sweet, and I loved her, Sister Helen, but she was always trying to get Slick to go back to church. She mentioned it every single time she came to visit us for the next, oh, fifty-plus years.

After the wedding, some of Slick's friends wanted to drive us around the town square of Ophelia, honking horns and having a kind of shivaree, but I didn't go in for that kind of thing. Drawing attention to yourself is a sure way to get hurt, I always think. That's another thing that I like about birds: they are timid. But they also don't always recognize predators and don't often learn about them until it is too late, because they are trusting. And just like there are all kinds of people, there are all kinds of birds. An albatross can't just jump into the air like a pigeon. I'd heard too much over the phone lines, and heard too much directly from the birds, to ever trust anyone.

CHAPTER 8

Little Ophelia seems such a treasure to me now, and so do all the places around us, in ways they never did before: the sweet little abandoned places to the north: Trinity Springs, of course, the dearest spot of all of them, but also Dover Hill, Indian Springs, and Williams; the places off to the south where all the rich visitors came: French Lick and West Baden; the practical towns to the west where it all went suddenly flat; and the places further on in every direction where we went all the time: Indianapolis, Louisville, and Evansville were the closest, each about two hours' drive away.

Fear of different people is so easy, isn't it? Now that I'm here, I realize that I've carried around more fear than I needed to, like a huge sack of rocks. But those larger cities did make me afraid, and it was the black people all gathered together in the middle of them that made me so. There, I've said it. They told me a few days ago, *"If you said it, you can shed it,"* so I guess I'm trying to shed it. Yes, I was afraid of black people. Birds are afraid of differences, too, and they taught me that very clearly. And dogs are naturally, meaning by *nature*, racist. Doesn't that have some meaning somewhere in our lives? I never wanted to be that person who pointed out that we are from different races, but of course we are, aren't we? I can no more understand another race than they can understand me, but I don't have to look back at my life and think anything about race and they probably do. I never suffered because I was a little wisp of a white girl. There was plenty of us.

As kids we ate things all the time that weren't good for us, and when we grow up we still do it because it gives us some comfort. It is the same with fear. All that fear is put into us. We eat it like a big piece of pie and it comforts us every time we bite into it. I'm not proud to say that I avoided downtown Indianapolis or Louisville because of black people, but that's how it was for me. How did we make them feel when we would drive our cars toward Monument Circle and lock the doors when we saw them crossing the street near us? That must have felt horrible, but we did it. We would go to the big shopping malls around the city, like over at Eastgate, only because they had fewer black people in the suburbs and it made us feel better to just go somewhere else so as not have to say that. All of Slick's Indianapolis nieces and nephews went to school with black people all the time, and they thought we was crazy or mean or racist for being afraid. But I just couldn't help it.

CHAPTER 9

Daddy used to hunt birds out in Trinity Springs, but Mama would never let him shoot or trap any birds that mated for life; she refused to dress or eat them, so over time he only ever brought home eating birds. There was still wild turkey and grouse in Indiana in those years. You could never say my daddy was a racist, not in the way they call people that now. But he and his buddies did used to try to run off the gypsies that was always gathering around the falls or in the state parks, and they roamed around the river towns, also hunting birds and anything else they could kill. I remember seeing them around the train station one time and they terrified me; they had a whole long line full of dead birds hanging off their cart. My, that's seventy-five years ago or more, but I think it made me afraid of strangers. Daddy and Mama were always telling us to avoid the gypsies. If we came up on them when we was playing anywhere, we were just to run the other way and come tell them so they could call the sheriff. I think I heard them a few times, always around the river, but I don't remember ever seeing them, do I?

I know from losing Daddy that you can't lose something you never had. I was so young when he was taken from us that I never felt I knew him at all, and we had almost no pictures of him. The ones Mama had she couldn't stand to look at, so we put them in a box where they've stayed to this day, somewhere in my house. I have trouble remembering him now, too, but I do know that one of the things I'm going to find out here is what really happened to him. Mama never did believe what they told her.

There was just too many shiftless characters around the trains in those years, too many things happening that couldn't be explained as normal. There was the story they gave us at the time, but as the years passed feelings changed, like a tree that stays the same but grows new branches. I couldn't rightly remember the day myself. I was young, true, just eleven or twelve, so it was during the Great War and just before the Pinnacle, but all those memories are jumbled into one muddle for me now.

Daddy was a contractor, so he did whatever work was available. They told us Daddy was hit by something that fell off a train. They was moving some gypsum from somewhere close by and Daddy was helping unload some other part of the train, and when he walked by the car loaded with gypsum, a support gave way and crushed him. We didn't know he was going to be unloading anything. Mama and I were on the train coming back from Seymour, where she'd bought me that year's pair of shoes. I knew the moment the train pulled into Ophelia and they wouldn't let us pull into the station that something awful had happened. We had to step off the train at least two blocks from the station, which felt so strange because the station was second nature. The preacher was on the platform with the sheriff waiting for Mama. I can still hear the way he said, "Beulah, I have very sad news."

He walked us to his house by the Baptist church, and his wife kept me outside and I showed her my shoes while Mama talked to the preacher. You could hear her awful crying all over town. They never let us see Daddy's body. They told her he was crushed by whatever fell on him and we couldn't stand the sight of it. Mama accepted that at the time, but I know that over her life she felt she should have seen him, should have tried to find out what really happened. But in those days you accepted things as they were, and the grief was so strong that it makes you say yes to things you wouldn't rightly do. Nobody has told me how long I'll be here, but they've made it pretty clear that it's temporary. I'm eventually going to go to some other place. I hope I don't have to go back there. I feel now like I felt then about the train station in those years after Daddy: it was really just a place for leaving and arriving, but it also became such a place of such loss and sadness that I couldn't hardly take it.

I was surprised at how much they know here and how much they write down for me. When I first got here, they gave me a little bit to read about Ophelia. "I lived there my entire life and there is nothing I don't already know about the place!" I laughed as they gave it to me. But then I read it. It was filled with things I either didn't know or didn't give much mind to if I ever did.

Ophelia, Indiana, sits in the lower part of the state of Indiana atop hilly deposits of an ancient glacier that swept the northern part of the territory completely flat and featureless. Lower Indiana is verdant in spring and summer, with rolling hills and rocky features randomly interrupted by clapboard houses. The most solid of the local buildings are churches, whose unsynchronized bells can be heard around the small valleys in echo. There is a three-block main street out of which other roads tentacle toward farms. Up the steepest hill of the settlement is a courthouse, with huge elm trees in front labeled with the dates of lynchings that had drawn huge crowds of many people.

I loved that beautiful hymn-word, *verdant*, and I know they used it because they knew I would like it. The report went on to talk about things I thought I knew very well: the Jug Rock, House Rock, so many covered bridges, most of which are gone now, the Pinnacle, Marengo Caves, and, of course, the river. I kept asking why I had to read all of this and they've always said, "You don't have to; but you are welcome to, if you'd like to understand. The more you can learn about something, the more you can tell the truth about it. We will only write something you can understand; you'll never be made to read something you can't comprehend." I thought that was interesting, but I still don't rightly know what they meant.

CHAPTER 10

I'd heard about the Archer lynchings my whole life, and I even thought Daddy and Mama had been there since they always remembered it in such horrible detail, like they had watched the crucifixion, but now I realize they weren't there at all. They just repeated stories they'd heard. I'd thought all this time that the Archer boys were black, thought their lynching was like so many others that we all heard about. But the paper they gave me, which I know must be right, said they was white boys from down around Princeton or Oakland City who got mixed up with a bad lot. They would go years doing nothing wrong, even pretending to be preachers, and when they needed money for something, they would drive up to little towns like Ophelia, blend in, gain trust, and then rob and murder people. They finally got put in the old jail and they had a trial and the judge was going to send them somewhere else for their sentencing. I don't rightly remember. But the people of Ophelia, Daddy used to say, would not stand for anything less than complete justice, so they formed a mob, broke into the jail, and hung the two boys and their dad from the big elm trees in front of the courthouse. There was professional photographers and everything. You see the photos and everybody is smiling like they are at a picture show. It was about twenty years before I was born.

Mama hated that they put signs on the trees. She thought it was an awful thing to have to remember them marauders and the bloodthirsty crowds that showed up to watch them die. She talked all the time about people in Ophelia who she was surprised would take part in something like that. "You think you know people you see every day, but you don't," she would say, and there were people she never spoke to again after the hangings. I think those trees in front of the courthouse were like Golgotha to her, and they brought to mind other things she didn't want to think about, like Daddy's death; and, I know it must be true, the thing that happened to me that I think must have been harder on her than anyone else. I haven't been able to talk about it yet since I got here, but I can feel it approaching in the distance like one of them old trains rumbling way out of town that you know is going to get there soon.

CHAPTER 11

I loved all birds, but in spite of what the family said about me, I wasn't dumb enough to think that all birds are nice. Some can be incredibly dangerous to people and many, like penguins, falcons, or hawks, are dangerous to other birds. Danger or no, I could join their sights and hear them if I really wanted to. I've heard the birds talking about many dangers over the years. The birds in our yard or at East Side Park can sense a predator within half a mile. They can sense everything: trains coming, dogs, cats of course, but also snakes and smaller critters we don't notice. They see every radio and television wave invisible to us. Cable TV was one of the best things to happen to the birds, but it was all canceled out by those awful phones that everybody felt they just had to have. I could never understand wanting to be able to talk to anyone anywhere at any time. Wasn't the greatest joy of life to *not* have to talk to people?

I knew my gifts with the birds were temporary, but I will say one thing about the phones near the end of my life: I'm so grateful for what I saw because even though it was scary, it was also strangely beautiful. It kept me entertained for many an hour, to see that vision of what the birds actually saw in the world, the gigantic grid of constantly pulsating radio waves. Doctors would look at me and say right out loud that I wasn't responding to them, as though I didn't hear them or didn't know I wasn't responding. Of course I wasn't, I was busy! I couldn't look at everything at once, and there was so much.

To some of the birds the radio pulses are every color imaginable. To some they look like X-rays in black and white. It must make them half crazy—I know it did me—but somehow the birds survive seeing all of that at once. Maybe they've found a way to make it beautiful. Sounds make waves. I could often see them as I connected people at the telephone office, but all birds have been seeing that for centuries upon centuries. How much more peaceful their world must have been before we developed radios, when the only things that radiated were natural. The differences between the birds were in how they chose to use what they saw. The birds I truly loved and tried to protect were the birds who tried to warn the world, and each other, of impending danger. I couldn't always tell what the precise dangers were, but I knew the birds knew. I learned one big thing from my forever day: that the world is now in jeopardy and something is malignant, exactly like they talk about cancer, and it started long ago. We are in great danger now. Maybe that's why they are keeping me here, so I can tell them. But I can't.

Bird songs always sounded to me like questions and answers; and for a long time I couldn't tell what they were asking and answering. I was content that there are things in life that I'm not supposed to know. My favorite birdsong was in the morning when I'd work in the garden, because that was the time of day when they were most vocal. I swear, too, that at work I could hear the birds trying to communicate through the telephone lines. The question-and-answer birdsong changed as autumn arrived, in the weeks before most of the birds disappeared for the winter. The birds that stayed high in the trees would talk to the ground birds, and the ground birds always answered. I wish I knew more about music, because I know that a real musician would be able to describe and understand the questioning and answering, because music did that all the time. I could pick out bird songs on the piano, but it sounded like nonsense to anybody else.

CHAPTER 12

When you go for years needing to say something but people just won't listen to you no matter what you do, it does awful things to you. Your body shrivels up like an old piece of fruit left on the porch. As horrified as I was to have seen this in so many of Mama's generation, the hardest thing for me was seeing it in my own bathroom mirror every morning. I knew something about Jerry Ballard that no one else knew, and I willingly let people *not* know it my whole life. I first noticed my body shriveling up a short time after my forever day, after Slick started getting bad. The thing I could never talk about around Slick's family, which meant I couldn't talk about it at all, was the Catholic Church.

Ophelia was surrounded on all sides by Catholic places. Mama used to say she didn't mind them so much, except that they brought the KKK around, which they sure did when I was little. At least we don't have to hear much about the KKK anymore. It was terrible when I was young, and they terrorized the places that were built to give Catholics such a stable feeling. You went to St. Meinrad, Ferdinand, or all the way up to St. Mary-of-the-Woods, and you felt you were in a permanent place, much more than you felt at any normal school that you knew would be torn down someday. Those places were so beautiful, so big, and they gave you such a feeling of peace. I was not a fan of the Catholics, but I will admit that pulling into the front gate of St. Mary-of-the-Woods was like entering heaven. There was a grotto there where you could just sit and pray, and I went with Slick while he did that. I listened to the birds, of course. The birds there were the happiest birds I ever heard, so the place must have been peaceful inside as well, 'cause the birds always knew things like that. Even though Slick didn't go to church anymore, he was obsessed with going to these Catholic places. We even drove all the way up to Rensselaer, halfway to Chicago, just to look at the chapel there, which was more of a cathedral.

St. Mary-of-the-Woods, where Slick's sister lived when she wasn't out teaching somewhere, also had the scariest thing I'd ever seen, and I could never see why Slick nearly always made us go down there: the crypt. It was under the church there, Immaculate Conception, which was such a beautiful place that I could not for the life of me understand why they needed a crypt when there was a perfectly good cemetery on the outskirts of the campus. Slick never wanted to go there but he always had to drag me down to the crypt. You got there by a long stairway next to the church, and there was always an ancient nun sitting at the top waiting to let you into the crypt. She would ask us if we desired to see the *Pietà*, as they called it, and every single time Slick would say yes, and she would ask us to wait while she went downstairs to turn it on. It was the most haunting thing you ever saw, worse than any statue of Jesus I'd ever seen. It had little lights in it that made it so graphic, made the blood look like it was flowing. Slick would get silent in front of it, and then he would cry as though he had done something wrong. The statue never made me cry; it just gave me the willies.

CHAPTER 13

We were just Birdie and Slick, always thought of together for almost the whole century. From far back everybody gave me bird presents, so I've always had to wonder if my special way with birds was because of my name or if Mama somehow knew my ways before I was born and that's why she named me that. Mama had some of them specialties herself, but she never used them, since she would have found them against God. They told me my voice would be the same here as it used to be. I always knew we had a forever day, but I just could never quite put the words together to explain it. I seemed to have several forever days, every few years or so, and that is still confusing because for years I thought you only got one.

Just now I'm on a day in 1973 that I'm not able to move beyond. I just cannot leave that day. I thought that was why they called it my forever day, but I'm learning more now and realizing that ain't so, either. I'm the one who first called it that, and that is strange to me, because I usually only repeat things others have said. In the end, though it is all foggy to me now, I did almost make it a full century, didn't I, right along with the real one? Am I remembering that right? All that newness that joined me into the world in 1900, if I'd only known! I thought everything would be so different here, but the parts I can so far figure out feel the same. I still have to explain to some that Birdie was not my nickname. Slick used to tease me about it all the time, back when he could still say it. I miss how he called me "Birdie-wordy" because I talked a blue streak whenever we weren't with strangers. It would surprise him that I find words easier now than I ever did, and I'm starting to see that the answers are easier, too, but you still have to go looking for them and you still have to *ask*. Despite what everybody seems to think, it isn't peaceful here. I still have things I have to accomplish, things I didn't get done, and nothing changes those; you never get out of doing your work. Odd. I keep asking when I can see Slick and Mama and all of them. No answers yet.

CHAPTER 14

What fools all them Catholics are to think they are more powerful than the birds or the sea or the stars. Of course, I never saw the sea, never saw a seagull, though we did sometimes get ocean birds off their course in southern Indiana during the migration months. The world belongs to the birds, and we live here only because they've never decided anything different from that. But the time will come when they will have listened to enough nonsense, and they will just take their world back. When that time comes, there will be no stopping them. We—mankind, that is—are the biggest danger to the birds, but don't we realize they are also the biggest threat to us? After all, we killed off Dodo birds just for the fun of it, just for the joy of killing something that was no threat to anybody. I hated reading about the Dodo birds. I wish I could have met one!

The people who tell me things here say I blame everything on the Catholics, and they might be right. But them Rome-lovers tried all my life to get at my husband, to get us to come around to their way of thinking about the world, and I just would not. The Catholics want their church to be like a movie, with starring roles for some people and minor roles for others, and they wanted fans and popularity, things religion shouldn't want. We are the stuff of stars, all right, but not the Hollywood kind of stars, who I just know are never as interesting in person as the people they play in movies, though I never once met a movie star so I'm not so sure.

I like what people actually *do*, not just what they talk about doing, so when that Gene Shalit or people like him blather on about the movies, it just drives me crazy. From everything the birds have told me, we are from those real stars, the ones you see at night here in southern Indiana, so far from the big cities. We are made from the same things, so that means the planets and the moon are in my skin and in the bird's songs and everything that is alive. Isn't that the most amazing thing of all, that we are unique but we are all the same? That is where I cannot hazard a guess at religion. I just can't. Because they don't want us to all be made of star stuff. They want us to have been created specially, to have no relation to anything else, set apart. Doesn't that make us smaller? My special way with birds told me more than any Catholic, because the birds know all about what we are made of. They know the stars.

Being here, which is just a fancy way of saying I'm no longer *there*, and the biggest thing I've realized is how afraid I've always been, because fear just isn't something they feel here. I always knew that fear wasn't a Christian virtue, since I heard that all the time as a little girl, but it wasn't what was practiced. I was surrounded by fear all the time, both my own and everybody else's. Fear has eaten a lot of my life, and I know I can't let that go on. It feels like I wasn't afraid of anything before my forever day but of course that isn't true, either. I was afraid of absolutely everything. It feels like such a waste now. But the more I can understand about why I was afraid, the better I feel.

CHAPTER 15

The lightning bug season is way too short in our hilly corner of Indiana, but it is my favorite season no matter how long it lasts. Them bugs make our yard into a fairyland, and the amazing thing is that the birds leave them alone. I've never quite understood why. I guess they taste awful. I've seen a few bats try to eat them, but even they spit them right out—but bats surely aren't birds. There was a little hill at the back of our yard, and nobody ever knew this, but I could go back there on summer nights and pretend I was on a stage. I would wave and hear the applause in my mind. I would pretend I was a dancer or pretend that people loved to hear me play the piano. Them fireflies, if you squinted your eyes just right, were like thousands of little cameras taking my picture from way off in a big theater, bigger than the Pantheon, Odeon, or the Murat, the big places I went to when I was younger. I never told Slick or Mama that I did that. It would have embarrassed me to death if they'd known. Since I got here, they make me talk about all of these things, or maybe I started talking about it all because I got here. That part is still foggy, but things here are getting clearer every day. Why on earth they want to know about things I did seventy-five years ago is beyond me, but they keep on asking and I keep on not telling.

CHAPTER 16

I never did care for that Alfred Hitchcock's weird movies, especially when he made that one about birds. I couldn't bear to ever see it because I don't like scary movies—and I certainly did not want to be scared by birds. Birds was the one thing in my life I wasn't ever afraid of, and I'll be darned if I would let that fat Englishman make me so. Of course, birds could be dangerous and scary if they ever decided to be, but they have no need for it; it is only humans who are cruel for the fun of it. The birds were my gods: they see everything and never interfere. They fly around amazed and confused by our choices, because they are almost always against what we should be doing. How could they not be? I always knew what was coming just by listening to them, but no one would ever listen to *me*. Hitchcock made that movie where the girl was stabbed in the shower by the boy who stuffed birds, so I know Hitchcock was a sick puppy and I was not about to put any of my money in his pocket. It is just awful to think that people would look at a bunch of birds and see fear, and awful to think that a movie could do that. Birds are the most beautiful living creatures, and there are many more of them than there are of us.

CHAPTER 17

I was mad at the starlings for ages because one summer years ago, I was doing laundry outside and I took my wedding ring off because of the harsh soaps. I put it on our picnic table and darned if one of them starlings didn't see it shining in the light and carry it right off in front of my eyes. If I'd had a gun at that minute, I would have shot that bird to get my ring back—and I am not a person who ever believed in shooting birds. I was beside myself. I couldn't very well afford to buy another wedding ring. Hell, we could barely afford the one I had. And I didn't have the heart to tell Slick that I didn't have it anymore. I worried myself into such a frenzy that day, finishing up the laundry and worrying about my ring, that I nearly forgot I needed to clean the birdbaths, and it was such a hot day. As I tipped the first birdbath over to clear out the old water, I noticed something shining in the late-afternoon sun. Darned if that starling hadn't just dumped my wedding ring in that birdbath. Imagine that! I fretted all day over absolutely nothing, since the bird took it and gave it back, and if I hadn't seen that starling carry it off, I might never have noticed he'd brought it back to the birdbath. Life is so funny that way. But it was proof to me, too, that you should never shoot a bird, because if I'd shot it, my wedding ring would have landed God knows where; as it was, it brought it right back to me in a place all of my local birds knew I would find it.

CHAPTER 18

Jenny was a curious little girl to me, such a smart little tomboy. One of the perks of being old *and*, let's face it, not being there anymore, is not being afraid to name a favorite, and Jenny had always been my favorite since she was very young. I loved dressing her up in some of my extra doll clothes, though as she got older she liked to dress in boy's clothes for a while before I put a stop to that. I was always more comfortable with the nieces than the nephews, and it wasn't just Stevie. Jenny was gentler toward the world right from the start, like Slick. I felt gentler and more kindly just being around her. Jenny had a curiosity about everything. I was bound by an invisible duty to treat them all equally, and I tried to do that, but it was hard not to favor her. She was a little girl who didn't have tantrums or have suspicions about people. She was the picture of innocence, so if Stevie had taken any of that innocence from her I don't rightly know what I would've done. Jenny also had a knowing quality that I recognized. Maybe she also heard the birds. I wasn't quite sure at that time, and I'm trying to get clearer about it now, but I do think she might have. Stevie never heard a bird in his life, but I tried. God knows I tried.

CHAPTER 19

Slick's family was so big that it was hard to keep track of all of them. Through the '50s, as they were all raising their families, I did a lot of babysitting because we didn't have kids of our own. I loved that. And we all got together a lot as a family, and it was fun, at least when they didn't talk about being Catholic. But something shifted once those kids got into high school and started leaving home. When I was young, most people didn't run off to college and if they did, they tended to come back to Ophelia or somewhere nearby to use what they'd learned. But kids changed in those years. Most of the nieces and nephews that came along after the war wanted to go to college and live far away from their parents. I just couldn't understand it. I could no more have left Mama than I could fly right now, and I'm one of the people in the world who understood what it meant to fly, because I could see it and feel it. I got to a point in the '60s where I couldn't go to high school graduations because they upset me so, knowing that all the families would likely be broke up. I always felt it was better to stay close to home where there was a lot less danger. I'm waiting, though, for some smart person here to point out that all the dangers I faced were as close to home as they could have been.

Some of the younger parts of the family were more stay-at-home like mine had been. Unfortunately, other than Stevie, they weren't the ones I wished had stayed around. Slick's sister-in-law Hedy kept all her kids home after high school, not a one of them went to college. They somehow all turned out as sweet kids but I sure don't know how. Hedy was as bad as Gerry—and that is saying something, let me tell you. For a few years in the early '60s, Hedy worked with me at the telephone office. She worked out front collecting bills in the new office, after we left the old exchange. She was a fine one for that job! Everybody knew she stole things all over town. Couldn't keep her hands off anything. I kept an eagle eye on the books whenever Hedy was around, because I knew she would walk off with whatever wasn't nailed down. Stevie was pigeon-toed so I was all over him about that. That Gerry, his worthless mother, didn't seem to care at all.

Hedy always claimed she was named after Hedy Lamarr but as usual, that was total lie. She did not have one thing in common with that gorgeous creature. Oh my Lord, Hedy Lamarr was the most beautiful woman who ever lived, I tell you. People went on and on about Elizabeth Taylor but she did not have one thing on that Hedy Lamarr. But I was always upset when my sister-in-law Hedy claimed to have anything in common with the real goddess. Oh, she made me so damn mad sometimes. Well, all of the times.

Slick and I only ever went as far west as St. Louis, where he took me for our twenty-fifth wedding anniversary to a baseball game. We stayed at a motel near the Shriners Hospital, not too far from downtown, and I was absolutely scared to death the whole time. Oh my Lord, I think we was the only white people in that whole motel and sometimes I felt like we was the only ones in the whole darn town! When I worked at the telephone office, I met a number of black people and I always liked them, but, well, you can't just throw out the way you was raised, can you? I didn't like crossing the Mississippi River because it made me feel so far away, and I don't like big bridges! They scare me to death because I always think they are going to fall down. Sometimes they do, too: I saw on television a big bridge in Washington State that swerved and buckled, and then tumbled right down into the water below! Nightmare!

Traveling aside, I keep trying to explain to everyone here that my forever days always happened at *home*. That's where I was happy and that's the place I never wanted to leave. I know lots of people who had a fine time traveling around the world, lots of folks who drove to Las Vegas from Indiana, and some that even went by plane. You'd never get me on one of them huge airplanes that are so heavy they are just begging to fall out of the sky, and I certainly would never go to Las Vegas. It looks like it is full of gamblers and whores, and filled with people who smoke and curse. I can't imagine throwing away hard-earned money on that.

And the shows they went there to see: Frank Sinatra and Sammy Davis, Foster Brooks, Dean Martin, and all of them people you saw on television. They all seemed to be drunk all the time, and I just know in their live shows they must have cursed. Slick loved to watch Dean Martin roasts on Thursday nights. There was one just near my forever day, I think it was of Johnny Carson, and I must say I did enjoy that because even though I knew Johnny smoked and drank, I didn't think he cursed. And they at least had the sense not to have that awful Don Rickles on to roast Johnny. I couldn't stand Don Rickles. I liked Jonathan Winters and Rich Little, since they could really entertain and didn't have to resort to cheap cursing. I could watch Rich Little all day long and never get tired. I mean, that man can sound and even *look* like anybody. I never seen anything like it. And that Jonathan Winters just makes me roll on the floor, too, but nobody does that like Paul Lynde. Lordy, he was just the funniest man on the face of the earth. I loved him. Slick liked that old drunk Foster Brooks, but I just thought he was silly. Drunkenness is not funny. Paul Lynde, though, well, I would have gone about anywhere to see him, and I looked out for him on television, and I would plan our trips around him being on. *Hollywood Squares* wouldn't have been anything without him. He always looked as happy as a puppy with two peters. So many of the stars seemed so grumpy. What did they have to be grumpy about, for God's sake?

CHAPTER 20

I always felt so ashamed of not being as good a person as I could have been. I've lived long enough to realize why shame came so easy to me, as did guilt. If I'd been paying attention that long-ago day, my whole life might have been different. I used music and collecting to escape but I'm ashamed of that, too, because I never learned how to make music properly. My own ten-year-old niece could outplay me at the piano and I'd been doing it for sixty-five years at that point! I felt guilty about the birds, too, because whatever they've been trying to tell me, it isn't working. Until my last forever day, I couldn't understand them completely, or I was unwilling to hear what they were saying, so a lot of my life was about not being able to get there, either.

I tried always to remember that my connection to birds was a gift, but I had to sometimes wonder what the point was of such a useless gift. There was nothing I could do with it because no one was ever going to believe me, even after I figured out what they was saying, and by then I was old and nobody listens to an old lady. I was hoping that as I got older I'd be more able to just have some peace of enjoyment within myself, so I could at least lose the need to have people believe me. I think I might have that now.

CHAPTER 21

Before the second war, movies defined everything about my life. All through the '30s, which were also my thirties, we went to the Shawnee or The Ritz, and for special occasions we'd go to the Pantheon, several times a week. We saw absolutely everything, and I loved the musicals the most, which made me start buying song sheets of everything from the movies. We had all kinds of songs then: theater songs, popular songs, more-serious songs that girls sang in parlors or on the stages of the vaudevilles, movie songs, church songs of course, and we all knew so many of them. It was only after the war that a smaller amount of music got more popular, and everything seemed to shrink from that time.

The first song I remember little Jenny playing at the piano was a morbid little country song that got popular in the late '60s, "Honey," which was just like that song we used to sing when I was a girl, "Listen to the Mocking Bird." It was all about singing over a dead woman's grave. I swear, every time I go out to the hill to visit Mama, the same set of birds comes home to the great old trees nearby to sing to me and I think of that song. Sure as the world, those birds are singing that song. Well, little Jenny brought it to mind again for me when she would play for hours on our piano and sing those sad words about Honey. She didn't have the first idea what she was singing about, which just made it all the cuter.

CHAPTER 22

1925 was just an awful year for me. Unmarried at twenty-five! I baked two cakes to take to Floyd Collins when he got trapped in Mammoth Cave that year, because I figured everybody would be taking regular food and I thought he should have a cake or two waiting for when he got out, but he never did. I turned twenty-five and was still single. People around Ophelia were starting to talk. And above it all, we had an earthquake. Everybody said that earthquakes were because God was upset about some choice you made. Did I really choose? I feel like I wasn't given a choice. You just don't think about things like earthquakes in southern Indiana. That year changed me completely, because it was the year I met Slick. The magical quarter-of-a-century.

And the tornadoes in March of '25 shocked us all. They blew down the Heinz factory down at Princeton before wiping it and Griffin, neither of them very far from here, off the map. I don't know how Ophelia has been spared the tornadoes, but I read that it is the way we sit on hills, and the Pinnacle protects us. I can see why people believe that. The birds think differently: they think it is because we are being judged and our real judgment is still waiting. I am always going to believe the birds over people.

CHAPTER 23

I worked at the phone office in Ophelia all through the second war. I heard all of the calls. So much heartbreak. The calls from the War Department to some of the country houses that still didn't have home phones were the worst for me. I'd have to send a message to them to come into the phone office to ring them back, or give them an assigned time to take a call at a nearby house, all so they could hear that their son was never returning from Belgium or the South Pacific. 1944 was the worst, as a call seemed to come nearly every day. Not so much for Ophelia, but for all the surrounding towns. The phone lines got so confused in those years because there was so much info being passed around. And I was always afraid we would be bugged. I kept my ear open for that all the time, because the BOO, the Bureau of Ordnance, had been opened near the beginning of the war, and there was so many strangers in and out of there during the war years. They used our phone lines all the time and it worried me to death, because it would have been easy for a German or a Jap to spy on us through the phone lines. The things I heard through the lines during the war would have been very useful for them, but I watched the open lines like mad as a part of my own war effort.

There were days when I noticed the birds gathering on the lines in larger number than was usual, not quite like the later Kennedy day but related to that. There was a trunk-phone pole right by the railroad track by our office, and the lines spread out in all four directions from it. Very unusual. Over time I noticed that on certain days the birds would collect themselves on the line leading north, toward the depot, and I would always listen in especially at those times. The Catholic Church was calling the naval depot every day during the war, and whenever they did the birds would gather. Sometimes people would laugh at us having a naval depot in Indiana, so far from the sea. But the Navy had to have places to build their supplies, build their weapons, and all the support things needed to keep them going. The Catholics, in those days, were talking to some of the higher-ups at the depot, I guess knowing they would take it up higher, from 1942. I never could quite believe what they were saying, but I had to because I knew the birds were hearing it and taking it on. The Catholics were saying that the Krauts were rounding up Jews and killing them, and the Catholics were trying to get all kinds of Jewish families relocated into the States.

Needless to say, this was not a popular view to have in 1942. I mean, all our little towns were Catholic, and even though I'm as ticked off at the Catholics as anybody, at least I can see that all of our churches are Christian. The idea that they would bring a bunch of Jews over to live among us. It's gotten so you can't say anything like that because the minute you do, people will say you are just like the Nazis. I hated the Nazis as much as Winston Churchill did, but I'm also practical enough to know that a bunch of Jewish families plonked down into southern Indiana or working at the naval depot was just never going to fly. It wasn't *me* being against the Jews; I just know human nature. And the birds did, too. When the Catholics were on those calls, they would not stop talking to each other, would not settle down. It is funny to me. The birds sat around with all this knowledge and didn't do anything with it, because I know as surely as I know I am alive that the birds hear us. The birds need us to hear *them*, because if we could it would make a difference. The world would be better.

CHAPTER 24

It wasn't only that the birds sat on telephone lines. Owls loved to build nests inside of telephone poles, and I always wondered what they might hear. Funny, I was never able to communicate with owls. They are a breed apart from birds even though they are birds. The other birds don't seem to pay them much mind, even when their beautiful hoots sound all through the yard. Owls are so beautiful, so human, but they continue to terrify me because their eyes always feel like they see right through me to some truth I don't even know myself. It is always at that early time of dawn when the birds sing the most, because they are welcoming the day and checking on each other, that I am most able to hear and see what they are saying to each other.

CHAPTER 25

Now, after the war, once we found out what really happened over there, it took a long time to soak in that they had killed all of them Jews. How could people let that happen? I mean, they were all just trying to live their lives where they were born, weren't they? That's a far cry from the darn Catholics trying to move them all over here. Everybody knew Hitler was a madman, but he can't have done anything alone. The regular people in Germany, the ones like me who worked at phone offices, or the ones who knew how to listen to the birds, had to have known and not done anything. There had to have been birds at those camps, and somebody must have heard their cries. I know I was wrong to feel what I did during the war, and I was wrong not to listen to the birds about the Jews, but I can't be made out to be a bad person for it. They were my feelings, and feelings just are. They aren't wrong.

And where was our God? God was God, of course, but what kind of God lets the Krauts kill so many Jews, or lets the Japs shove bamboo under priests' fingernails? The way all of these churches talk about Him it must mean the Devil is a God, too, or maybe just a God who got ticked off by something and he was going to use the rest of time to get even. That's the simplest reason I liked salt and pepper shakers: they came in pairs. We feed some birds and we eat others. That is just the way of things. Oh, they asked me about all of the salt and pepper shakers, can you imagine? Why would anybody care about that? I'll get to it when I get to it, but I guess I'll tell them.

CHAPTER 26

I never understood people who love words more than they love music. For that matter, why do people love words so much, anyway? I mean, anybody can come up with a few words that sound nice, but it is the way people act that makes a difference to the world. Why wouldn't a person love actions over words? A person is the total of what they did in their life, not what they talked about. I had plenty of people over my whole life who could talk a blue streak, and I liked what they said, but as much as not, they didn't act like they talked. The thing I loved the most about the way the birds talked to each other was that they didn't lie. They didn't know how. They said exactly what they needed to: danger first, then food, then anything else. I loved that and wished for more people like that.

The farthest away I ever was from Ophelia was when we went to Chattanooga and the Smokies back in the '50s. There was a mountain up around Chattanooga that they said you could see seven states from, but all I could see from the lookout were the birds. Oh my, but they had just wonderful birds down there!—and some of them weren't the birds we had in Indiana. They came from all over the place, like they was on their way to somewhere, and they probably were. I know Florida is supposed to be real nice, but that was too far away for me. They even had some Florida birds in Chattanooga, can you imagine? I met some types of birds there that I never would have otherwise, but I didn't like being away from home. I liked our home birds the best.

CHAPTER 27

We was driving around Mitchell early one morning, waiting to get into Spring Mill State Park for a sale they was having on pictures. I thought they might have something I could hang above the piano, but all they ended up having was expensive real paintings that I didn't like. They charge hundreds for them! Some of them were pretty enough but they were just too high. Anyway, we drove around. I hadn't been in Mitchell in years, so we looked around at everything. Gus Grissom's house where he grew up, the houses of friends I knew. Went to the cemetery since I knew a lot of people from Mitchell.

We was driving around the cemetery when I noticed a shoe box along the side of the road. That ain't something you see every day, and it reminded me of a story I'd read about finding a bunch of money in a shoe box. So I made Slick stop so we could pick it up. I was such an idiot. I was just sure that was going to be a big box of cash. Well, I brought that box into the car and Slick pulled away. I opened it up and found it was an entire shoe box full of dog shit! Somebody collected the dog shit from the cemetery and put it in a box! The smell was just not to be believed. I screamed for Slick to stop the car so I could throw it out, and the moment the fresh air hit my face when I opened the door, I retched all over the place. I can laugh about it now, but it was one of the worst days of my life. Never pick up a shoe box. Oh my Lord, it was awful.

I kept trying to find the perfect picture to hang over my piano. It was the biggest wall in the house so it had to be something nice. It seems like every weekend Slick and I would drive somewhere so I could look for a picture. Ayr-Way, Kmart, and Sears usually carried big pictures, and I scoured every one of them for years. I liked pictures of mountains, hopefully with a few birds painted in, too. They was just copies of paintings, I know, like big posters that were framed, but I loved them all the same. They was twenty-five or thirty dollars, so I didn't mind changing them every few years. Sometimes the kids would tease me about not getting a "real" painting, but I didn't care. I think I loved our trips to those big stores as much as I did the paintings. I lived for those blue-light specials, because they were really special back when they started, before people started acting so crazy. Shopping was fun back then.

CHAPTER 28

Slick could keep silence for years. It was just how he chose to live, and it was sure the Catholic way. He wasn't ashamed of anything. It's just that things didn't occur to him. I wasn't much different; it took me a full ten years to convince him that he should put in snacks for sale in the station so the boys from the Catholic school wouldn't go to the Arrow. When I first suggested it, Slick said he didn't want to take any business from the Arrow. Then I realized he was really scared of the priests. I couldn't rightly understand it, until I realized that he'd grown up not having the luxury of having *talked* to priests like the boys do now. For years, priests weren't shepherds tending flocks. Slick could never see what I saw: that the only job of the priests, all the way up to the top of Rome, was to create future Catholics, and they would stop at nothing to do that. I saw it all from my little distance, but Slick could never see it, so I never brought it up because I didn't want anybody in the family to think that the reason he didn't go to church had anything to do with me. It didn't. He made his own decisions.

So many of them priests, and Slick's sister the nun, tried to explain to me the great fullness of God. Well, I will tell you the only creatures I know of who understand the fullness of God, and you'll know it yourself by now with all I've already told you: the birds. Birds can rise up on the wind and see for miles. They remember everything about their surroundings—where they hid food, where the predators are, where they can find water. They find a new place to live every season using just the temperature of the air and the direction it is coming from. You show me any person in the world who has those talents and then talk to me about the fullness of God.

CHAPTER 29

The priests came and went so fast over the years that I couldn't keep up and remember them all. When I spend time in my memory now, which seems to be all I can do, they all seem like the same man. Maybe in Ophelia we always got the newly ordained ones right out of St. Meinrad, on a short little stop on his way up the church ladder. I don't know. But I do know we had a long stream of Charlton Hestons come through town and they didn't ever stay more than a few years. Slick was practically fawning over some of them, which I guess is just what happens with Catholic boys when they get older. I thought his brothers were sort of the same way but now I'm not so sure. I think Slick was much more so than his brothers, which was always odd for me because Slick was the one of all of them who *didn't* go to church. All of his family blamed me, behind my back, for him not going to church, since I was the only one who married into the family and didn't convert. A lot wasn't talked about openly; it was just expected of you.

But anybody I ever knew who grew up in the Catholic Church was hooked forever. Whether they attended or not, the influence of the church was felt in almost every part of life, like a mother's love or some childhood accident you can't never forget. If the church didn't seep in, Catholics found a way to seep out. I'm learning now what went on in those days, especially during the 1950s and '60s, but it is still like looking through cheesecloth. Every day, though, it gets clearer if I want it to.

CHAPTER 30

The customers at the station, especially back in the 1950s, were forever bringing Slick gifts. You never knew what they would bring at Christmastime. Fruitcakes, of course, which I never minded because I could live on them fruitcakes, but it was the weird food they would send along, especially when it was perishable, that I could never understand. One year somebody gave us a pound—an entire *pound*, mind you—of Limburger cheese. We couldn't have eaten even half of that cheese even if we'd had big parties, which we never did. I opened it up and the smell was so horrible that Slick took it outside and left it for the neighbor's cat. I was afraid that cheese would kill the poor cat and I said so. Slick said I was foolish and, "Birdie, that cat will have to lick its own ass for an hour to get the taste out of its mouth." He was always saying things like that and it would embarrass me to death, but that never did a thing to make him stop. He would just keep saying those things!

At the telephone office I was always able to listen in to people's business, but I didn't often hear more than that. Slick, though, was always making idle chat with people, so he was always the jokester. I was embarrassed by most jokes, because I just didn't understand them or they were too racy for Slick to be telling. He had all of his favorites that I heard a thousand times, but they always make me cringe when he'd tell them: "If a couple is married in Kentucky and they move to Indiana and get a divorce, are they still first cousins?" "Why are the Baptists opposed to premarital sex? Because it can lead to dancing." It took me years to get the Baptist joke, and by the time I did I was so embarrassed it took me that long to understand, I wouldn't laugh at it.

CHAPTER 31

The station was owned by some oil man in Humble, Texas, wherever that was, but Slick got hired to run it shortly after we got married. We never saw the owner, though he called every few years and you sure couldn't say he was humble, if that's even a real place. He did call us in the '60s and gave us a tip on an oil well he was going to drill not far from Ophelia. People don't think of Indiana as having oil but we do, or we did. I don't think they are finding much more of it around these parts, but there was some wildcatting after the war and we sank thousands of dollars into the wells. We made some money from them, too, though never enough to retire on like they promised us.

For years and years we had the only gas station in town, and it was at a crossroads, too, the end of a north–south highway and on a big east–west highway, so there was a lot of traffic. I couldn't believe it took until the 1960s for there to be any competition, and it didn't change our business one bit. The people who came to us stayed with us. Through the war, with Slick in Wisconsin, I kept it going by hiring local boys who couldn't get drafted for some reason, and I got very good at recognizing the shiftless ones. I had to watch those boys like a hawk even though I was so busy during the war with working at the telephone office and keeping the station going. They thought they could pull something over on me, but I didn't ever let them. Even after Slick came home and started running the station himself, I kept a close watch on it all because he was such a target for somebody to take advantage of him. He was sweet to everybody and he trusted absolutely everyone. I didn't trust anybody, truth be told. And I was extra protective of Slick because I knew how vulnerable he was down there on the highway exposed to strangers. He would have struck up a conversation with Adolf Hitler himself if he'd pulled in for gas. He could never conceive of the dangers because he never heard the birds, like I did.

CHAPTER 32

After a few years, when I would leave work I'd walk over around the station. I'd stop in the Arrow for a cup of coffee, and from a certain table there I could see Slick over at the station but he couldn't see me. I guess some people would say I was spying on him but I was really just protecting him without him worrying about knowing it.

It always bothered me that the Arrow kept its mitts on the young ones, selling them snacks after school. They made a killing on selling snacks! So I was happy to take their money at the station instead, and let the richer folks in town eat their lunches and dinners at the Arrow. I could see them boys over there every day after school, buying up the snacks and talking to Slick. Sometimes he even let the older boys help him with the cars if they had interest. A lot of the boys from Ophelia had the touch for working on cars—better than Slick ever was, frankly. Slick touched the boys on the shoulder all the time but I didn't think a thing about that, since it was all out in the open and it was just buddy stuff. A few times, after a long talk with Slick in the office, he would even hug a boy as he left. But I knew nothing worse than that ever happened, because I knew where Slick was every minute of every day. He called me when he was fixing to come home every night because he had all of the cash with him in the car. We decided to have a plan in case anybody ever tried to rob him, so he'd phone when he was ready to leave, and five minutes later I'd hear him pull into the garage. For all the years we were together, I knew where he was every minute, so I know that the things they are trying to get me to see are not true. I don't see the use of them even if they are true, because there's not a thing I can do about them now, is there?

CHAPTER 33

Turns out that 1973 was about the last year that service stations existed at all, as people started opening "self-service" stations in Indiana around that time. I could not believe that anyone would want them. A service station took care of everything for you: windshield, oil, whatever might be ailing your car, and Slick would sit and talk to you besides. I knew people, and I didn't think anybody would want to get out of their car in the dead of winter to fill it with gas and clean their own windshield. Slick loved that station and he could talk to anybody. Even the priests and the boys from the Catholic school would come into the station and talk to him, even though Slick hadn't set foot in the church for years. Before long people were building "convenience stores" at every gas station, places that looked just awful even while they all looked alike. Why in the world would you need to buy milk or pop at a service station? But people sure did. I'll bet I listened to "Tie a Yellow Ribbon Round the Ole Oak Tree" a thousand times that year. Just loved it. Wally Cox died and that just about killed me, as I always loved him when he was on TV and he was so young. At least when Noël Coward or Granny on *The Beverly Hillbillies* died—I never did learn her name—it didn't take me by surprise because they had been around for years and years.

CHAPTER 34

Then came my forever day. We all have a forever day, and if you are lucky, like me, you have a few. Mine came every fourteen years or so, for reasons I haven't been able to figure out yet. I haven't been able to move out my last one and I'm not totally sure I want to. It was the last happy time I can remember before all of the bad things started. And there was no relief from it after that spring of '73, when everything started to feel like that glacier they made me read about: life started moving slowly even though it was fast, and events in my life suddenly seemed to flatten everything in their path, and then dumping their debris into little piles that I couldn't budge. I don't know if I'm ever going to be able to move out of that day, and nobody has made me yet, so I won't. I've seen that some people stay in their forever day for as long as they possibly can, which must mean there are some that never leave them. Others seem to happily move on. Nothing seems regular here, especially after I spent so much time over there trying to do whatever is supposed to be regular.

This forever day was my last normal day. Jenny was spending the night. Slick was still himself. We went down to the Dairy Master and a carhop gave us wonderful big tenderloin sandwiches with french fries, then we went home to watch television and walk Ginger. The children were fine. I cleaned the bird feeders and washed the birdbath. I can still hear how happy the birds were that day.

CHAPTER 35

When we had little Jenny staying with us, we let her watch the TV. I always let Slick watch what he wanted, since I was never much interested in nighttime programs. Jenny would spend most weekends with us in those precious few years when she was still a child, usually staying from Friday until after *The Wonderful World of Disney* on Sunday night. That girl always got so blue late Sunday afternoon, but *Disney* usually got her in a better mood. Friday nights were the best, because she generally came to us right after school and her parents, Slick's brother and sister-in-law, always played cards on Friday nights. I never understood the fascination with playing cards, but Slick and I were the outsiders in the family on most everything. They all played every weekend: poker, gin rummy, euchre, bridge for the ladies if the poker games got too rough-and-tumble. When they all got together on Saturday nights, usually in Indianapolis, the poker games were like little wars, yet they would all get up on Sunday morning and sit in a Catholic church like nothing had happened. They would gamble with real money, money they didn't have, and they would smoke and drink through them games, sometimes going through three bottles of whiskey, so after a while we stopped going. We just decided it was best for us to do our own thing.

I loved the Friday and Saturday nights in those years when little Jenny was so often with us, like a real daughter but without all the headaches; one temper tantrum and home they go! But unlike Stevie, Jenny wasn't one for tantrums. She was as sweet a little child as you could find, old before her years. I'm sure she's a big reason that my forever day is stuck in April of 1973, because there is a lot to hold it there. We watched Elvis on television that month. I wasn't sure we should let little Jenny see him, but she wanted to so badly, so did Stevie, that I allowed it. I actually enjoyed seeing Elvis, myself, and he wasn't nearly as dirty as I thought he would be. The kids all loved him. I never understood the appeal and I didn't care for his music, but by 1973 he could hardly be called new anymore, and he did put on a good show.

The Vietnam War was on television every night, and Slick watched it all, but I couldn't bear to see that. The last American soldier in Vietnam came home just before my forever day; I'll never forget that. Too big to really grasp. Lyndon Johnson died that winter, obviously as upset by the abortion decision as the rest of us. Who in the world thinks that killing babies should be legal? Of course, I wasn't one to talk, but I don't think things are quite the same today as when it all happened to me. I loved *The Waltons* even though it was sometimes so sad. I needed television to help me forget, and *The Waltons* was too much like my growing-up time to be totally happy to watch. Still, they did it well. M*A*S*H was just awful. I can't watch any war programs, and I didn't like the way they joked about important things.

Some prisoners of war was interviewed on television, and you just can't figure that any human could treat someone like that. It was like hearing about WWII again and all the horrible things the Japs and Nazis did to people. Slick had a priest friend after the war who was a prisoner. He wrote a book about it that I still have somewhere, I think out on the covered porch. I tried to read it but I couldn't take it. They shoved bamboo shoots up under his fingernails, can you imagine? Slick felt so sorry for him that they visited a few times a month through the '50s, then that priest moved away to someplace out west. The priests were always coming and going. The thing is, I've met people like that right here who were, in their own way, just like those Nazis and Japs. No one believes that, but it is true. They might not have carried it out or been as organized, but given the right tools, they would have done the same thing: killed people who got in their way or didn't believe the same thing. I heard them on the telephone, just as hateful as could be, and always wrapped in the Bible or their church.

In April they opened them two huge buildings in New York City, the World Trade Center, whatever that was supposed to mean, and from the moment I saw them on television I had an uneasy feeling about them. Too big, trying to be as big as nature itself. I knew I would never see them with my own eyes, but they sure took a lot of pictures of them. The birds hate tall buildings, and they were very upset by the World Trade Center. They all talked about it. It was the spring for big buildings. Sears opened the tallest building in the world in Chicago, which Slick wanted us to drive up and see, but I was not about to go to the top of such a tall building. What if somebody blew it up? The birds did not like these tall buildings interrupting the frequencies that they see all the time. No one ever thinks about the birds when they build these huge towers. On our slides we'd look at the Eiffel Tower in Paris, a place I knew I'd never see, and just imagine what that does to the poor birds over there!

CHAPTER 36

You know them flying dreams that everybody talks about now? I had my only one in my whole life right around the time of my forever day, and that was when it dawned on me that names have magic inside them.

I was going through old records on the porch and I found one I hadn't heard in a month of Sundays, Vera Lynn singing "The White Cliffs of Dover." Oh, that woman's voice just thrilled me, and I loved that song, the way she says "laaaawphter" instead of just plain old "laughter." I guess hearing the word "Dover" set off something in me, because it was the night after I found that record that in my dream I was running a country store someplace just like the one that used to be up in Dover Hill, and Carol Burnett of all people came in the store, turned into a werewolf, and I was so scared I *had* to fly to get away from her. She screamed, "Birdie! I'm going to kill you!" Then, in the dream, Carol took off and started chasing me through the air! She was a bird but she was also still Carol Burnett.

Maybe I never had need of another flying dream. I think people need to dream about birds and flying because it is something we know we will never be able to do on our own. Isn't that why we like Superman so much, not just because he punishes bad people but because he can *fly*? What about that story in some of my old magazines about the boy who made wings out of wax but flew up high too close to the sun and they melted? He tried to fly in the face of God and he paid the price for it. We all do that. We try to defy what God has designed for us, but right now I cannot figure out just what and why God has in mind for me. He's sent me confusing messages about it for my whole life. We think about heaven and wings and angels, and I think we just assume that we are airborne once we leave the earth, but I know otherwise now.

I was working at the telephone office on the Sunday the Japs bombed Pearl Harbor. I'd never heard of the place before that day. I was also getting an early start on Christmas cookies in the little office kitchen, because we'd been at Slick's youngest brother's wedding the day before. Fudge and divinity and sugar cookies all needed to get done for the whole family, and with fifteen nieces and nephews between us then, that was a lot of baking. After the war we had nearly forty! There wasn't many birds left in Indiana by that early December, but there was still migrators coming through. Shortly before the attack started, before the exchange lit up like a Christmas tree, I looked out the window and saw what must have been a thousand birds clinging to wires, clumped around the four telephone poles I could see from up there. It took me a long time to realize what I was seeing and hearing in the birds, and I didn't fully know it then but now I do: they were listening.

They heard every prayer, every wish, every hatred, yet so far as I know they never did anything about any of it. I remember all those years ago when they first put up all of the telephone lines, and everybody noticing birds collecting themselves on the lines, and they all just assumed that they perched there because the lines were convenient. "If the lines hadn't been there, they would just perch somewhere else," was pretty much what everyone thought. Little did they know.

But I knew from my first days at the telephone office it was because birds can see what most other creatures only hear; because there was two times of day in those days that I could do it, too. Birds knew how to talk to each other long before we did. They've been doing it for millions of years and have it perfected. I hated when people said birds were stupid, though I was always too shy and insecure to ever correct anyone. When somebody said they had "laid an egg" when they failed at something, or when they called somebody a "birdbrain," it just made me so mad. Gerry, Stevie's worthless mother, was always saying to me that birds are stupid. She only said it to hurt me. I said to her, "Do you think you could find a different place to live every winter, just by following the air you were riding to get you there?"

The style now in my forever day is for the kids to show each other their middle finger. It is called giving somebody "the bird," which I just hate. Stevie just the other day told me that he had "flicked someone the bird" when they pulled out in front of him. Why do they have to bring birds into their silly world?

CHAPTER 37

Priests hovered around our house for years trying to get Slick back to church, since after the war he had never darkened their door except for his mom's funeral. I never said a word to him about it. I thought he'd go if he wanted to, even though I knew very well he didn't need or want to hear the latest pearl from Rome. I'd putter around our little dining room while the priests made their pitch to Slick. "Can we pray together?" they'd say, and he'd always say yes whether he wanted to or not. This one priest, a new one who was in Ophelia through most of the '60s into the '70s, talked like a farmer trying to buy back land he'd lost, and he walked like he had an egg broke up in him. I didn't like him.

"The church needs you, Slick. You haven't been a practicing Catholic since the end of the war," he'd say.

"I know that, Father, and I miss some of the regular nature of the mass, knowing what is coming next, saying the words. But I've got a busy life and my wife isn't Catholic," Slick said.

"What makes your life so busy?"

"You know. Work. A shopping trip on the weekends and then back to work. The station takes a lot of time," Slick said.

"Your wife could become a Catholic, you know."

I nearly went into the living room when he said that. Fat chance, bub! I thought.

"And your sister is a Catholic nun, is she not?" the priest said, as if to prove that Slick came from good stock.

"Yes, Father. She is. Has been for almost fifty years."

I remember when his sister Helen went into the nunnery. It was criminal how young those girls were when the convents took them in and turned them into nuns. I was always convinced that she had no choice in the matter, that she tried it out and then there was no escape. The church in those days was not about to give anybody a way out. Helen couldn't have been more than twelve when she started, because when we went to the mass that made her a nun she was only about seventeen, I think. Imagine doing that to a young girl! But she stayed there for her whole life. She's as sweet as she could be, but she drives me bats when she comes for a visit because I have to watch every little thing I say and have to hear yet again about how I should give away my mother's things, and yet again how Slick should be going back to church. When I married Slick, I had no idea how often I'd have to be around priests and nuns, that there was no avoiding them. They come right into the house whether you want them to or not!

The priest went on, "Slick, would you like to go to confession? It would do your spirit good."

I was proud of Slick's answer. "I don't have anything I need to confess, Father. I've done nothing wrong."

There was a sermon from years ago, must have been the '20s, that I always remembered, about grace. "What is grace?" the preacher kept asking us, as though he expected us to really answer. Like everybody else there, I went to the church for answers, not questions, but he must have been a good preacher because I still remember exactly what I was wearing when I heard it all those years ago. I remember feeling that grace meant forgiving anything and everything, whether or not someone asked you. Who can really do that?

I know, though, that I have to find grace for my own life, because nothing is ever going to be just handed to me without any work. But who is going to give me this grace? Slick showed a huge amount of grace through every moment of our life together. He forgave me so many things when most men would have just run the other way. He couldn't heal my wounds, and he knew it, but he embraced them, anyway, yet I treated him like a child even before he became a child again.

Slick's family all said grace before eating, but that moment of blessing a meal was what kept me from nearly all the family gatherings of my life. Oh, that horrible moment of silence before the grace made me so nervous, and I never knew what to do during the prayer itself. The family would robot their way through those words when I knew full well they didn't really know what they were saying. How could people say words every day that they didn't mean? Most of the family felt that saying grace brought the meaning and thankfulness of the meal into everybody's mind. My family never gathered in large groups except to attend funerals, and that was just fine by me. I liked seeing them one on one.

What kind of grace is there in a world that lets me be injured so young, and in a way that stopped me from being a woman? And what kind of grace is there in a world that takes Slick's mind away but leaves his beautiful heart open to be hurt every day? And what kind of world lets me live on and on, forever stuck in a time that will never come back? How do I forgive a world like that?

CHAPTER 38

Mama used to talk about diviners, and I wish I'd really listened to her when I was little. "Those are the people you want in your life, little Birdie, the divining people. They are the ones who look at trees and tell you what has happened in the world, because the biggest trees have been here since before Adam and Eve and they know. The diviners can read the language of the wind, just like the birds do when they find their winter home solely by the breath of God. They know the rocks and the soil and the air and the deeper meanings of fire and water. They can look at mountains and know how old they are, can you imagine? They can also look at the river flowing and tell you what it is like days upstream. There was a couple diviners who knew the 1913 flood was coming, but nobody listened. They can cut a little pathway across an anthill and tell you what is going on underneath it all. Those are the finest people in the world, my little Birdie." Oh, I remember Mama saying every one of those words. She could talk so beautiful.

I knew Mama was right about the diviners, but she was also too shy to admit that she was one, too. I knew by the way she listened to the best diviners of all, the birds. She could sit and listen to birdsong for hours and be as happy as pie. And she didn't know it, but a few days before she died, I saw her on one of the swings in the backyard with her back to me, and she was silently talking to a hummingbird. That hummingbird knew Mama and came around every day to see her, but that day she had that hummingbird hovering over a bowl of sugar water eating right out of her hand. I know that little bird helped her cross over. I could see it, could see what the little hummer was telling her, just the way that right now I can see what the birds see. I made Mama a hummingbird hat out of fabrics I had left over from spring dresses. She absolutely loved it and wore it every Easter.

I didn't think anybody would believe me about the birds, because I was so bad at divining anything obvious. I was terrible with words all my life, especially when I got anxious. When I was in my truest silence, though, I could hear what the birds was seeing and see what they was hearing, most especially after that last forever day, when something in my world shifted forever.

Me and words just did not get along at all. I'll bet I spent ten years trying to remember that stupid word *terra-cotta*, and then in the end I didn't need to remember it, anyway. I spilled some oil paint on my terra-cotta tiles that I bought in Indianapolis, high as cat's backs they were, and we put them on the old front porch when we closed it in. I tried every bit of cleaner in the world to get that darn paint off and nothing would get it out, so after a few years I decided I was going to have to replace the tiles and I wanted the same color but I could not for the life of me remember what it was. I went to every paint store in Louisville and Indianapolis just to look through all their color wheels to see if I could find the name. Nothing would make me remember that name. I would circle around it, dream about it, but I couldn't remember it.

The Carolina wrens were out in force that day, and their calls are the most beautiful, so it made me want to clean up the birdbaths all the more. Wrens have so many layers to their songs. There is always a song beneath the song that you have to really listen for. I doubt there is a better thing about being alive than hearing the late-afternoon wrens in Indiana when they are all going at it. It sounds to me like the music you must hear in heaven, after you get done listening to Patti Page and Kate Smith, of course!

Cleaning out the birdbath one afternoon, and refilling it, a bird flew right past my head. I could feel the rush of the air as it buzzed by, close enough to move my own hair on a windless day. And then, as sure as day, there the word was: *terra-cotta*. It was just like when I was a little girl and the birds would fly by my head and say "blaffer." It happened a lot but I never knew what *blaffer* meant. I guess I still don't. They tell me I will understand at some point.

Anyway, I finally remembered that terra-cotta word so I was getting ready to buy another set of tiles. Then the most incredible thing happened. It was a hot day and I was so heated and winded by clearing out the birdbaths that I thought I would die without an ice-cold Coke, so I gave Ginger her Hershey bar and I poured myself the biggest Coke I could manage, in one of them big Bell jars I had from Mama. I decided to go watch the birds from the new porch—we always called it new even when it got old—and as I walked out there I tripped, and that whole Coke went all over the floor, breaking the jar and scattering the ice and glass to hell and gone. It took me forever to clean it all up, but when I finally got rid of the hard stuff and wiped the floor clean, that Coke brought every bit of that oil paint up with it. That was my last Coca-Cola, I can tell you that. If that is the only thing that would bring up oil paint from a terra-cotta floor after years of trying other cleaners, imagine what that stuff does to your insides! Of course by that time I had probably drunk ten thousand Cokes, but I stopped cold from that day forward.

Slick explained to me that he knew men during the war who had trouble remembering certain words, and doctors had been able to help them. But I sure didn't need to see a doctor for that. I just could not remember this word, and trying to remember it would make my throat close up. As with everything else, Slick eventually stopped mentioning it, even as he drove me all over southern Indiana trying to find not just the replacement tiles, but to find the g.d. *name* of the color!

CHAPTER 39

Not long before my forever day, Jenny's parents took her to Evansville to see the Passion Play, the one from Germany that they tour every ten years or so. For months after, I've never seen a child more obsessed with anything. I was cooking us dinner one night, Slick was still at the station, and I didn't notice that Jenny had been quiet for a long time. Normally if she wasn't playing the piano she would be in the kitchen with me talking and helping out, so I thought something might be up. Stevie came in the back door, hugged me hello, and disappeared into the front room with Jenny. It took me a little while to notice that it was still quiet. I could hear them both muttering about something; very serious it was.

Stevie usually wasn't interested in anything Jenny did. I finally finished up enough to go see what they were doing, and you can't imagine what I found. Set up in front of the television, and all over the floor, was the crucifixion of Jesus Christ himself, except entirely made out of stuffed animals. That girl made a cross out of some kindling wood and crucified a little stuffed frog that I'd had around for years; put little tack nails right through his legs! And she'd found other little dolls, not my nice ones, thank goodness, to crucify alongside the poor frog, with all the other animals around as witnesses. She even had a teddy bear dressed up as Mary of Nazareth, and had drawn tears down the bear's face with a Magic Marker. It was all quite a sight that little pissant created, but I couldn't very well get mad at her, since she was just re-creating the Passion Play they'd taken her to see. That girl loved to put on shows, and this was just another show to her. She didn't do it to be blasphemous. I even thought for a minute that the nun might actually like it. At least Jenny was connecting to the Jesus story as a child. That's the way I thought about it, anyway. I tried not to laugh, so I asked her what she and Stevie had been doing.

"I had him help me with some of the construction. He made the crosses and I nailed everybody onto them," she said, almost giggling, like she was talking about playing with Barbie dolls or going to a regular kind of play instead of the reenactment of the Lord's torture and murder. Of course it wasn't so very different from what the Catholics did every weekend.

Her parents told me all about the play, and it sure affected them, too, and not just like they might talk about a show. They talked about it for weeks after. It had a funny name of a little town in Germany that had performed the Passion Play for years. Their ancestors had made a promise that if they were spared the bubonic plague or something, they would perform the play forever, and darned if that didn't bring them right to southern Indiana all these years later. I think putting Jesus on stage must be blasphemous, but you'd never know it from the way they all carry on about a bunch of actors playing him. The whole thing made me queasy, thinking about living through the crucifixion, even a fake one. I just couldn't take it. When you are trying to portray something so important, you have to be as true as you can, and how could any stage play possibly be true to the crucifixion? That's why I didn't like all those serious things they put on now. The movies used to be so fun. Now they all seem to want to preach about things and try to be realistic. I don't want things to be like real life. I want to escape real life sometimes, and there are fewer and fewer chances.

CHAPTER 40

I never had an easy relationship with the Lord, but at least I knew I was supposed to have one. I just could never figure out how to square going to church with living your life. I was brought up to believe in God, to believe that He created all. When I was little, nobody questioned anything about God, and we sure wouldn't have said some of the things they say now. A few years ago, one of my magazines came with a cover saying something about God being dead. My mother would have dropped dead all over again if she'd seen that.

People should realize how powerful their words are. Words bring things into being. They create. I know this. It isn't like one of the things we are asked to believe. It is a simple truth. Birds know it. They've listened to millions of years of words, and they've witnessed every act of creation from the words of humans. Every weapon ever used in every war started with words. Every hateful thing ever said was created by a word from some man—always a man. You have to be very careful with your words. At the telephone office, I heard people say the most horrible things, and you can't ever take them back once they've been said. They slither around like snakes waiting to strike again whenever a person might feel threatened.

Around here, you'd have to figure that everybody thinks the Catholics started Christianity. I don't rightly know, but I do think that knowing the beginnings of things should be important, because people are so slow to let go of things that you just have to figure that it means something to know how something started. I'm not smart enough to know how it all began, but I know from the birds that it was surely started by ambitious men who talked loud and knew what they wanted. These were men who were going to make sure their words were louder than the words of others.

I read in one of my magazines that the New Testament was written in Greek, which must mean something. I mean, if the Greeks were writing it long after Jesus lived in a language the man didn't speak, that would be like people right now writing about the first war, whether they were there or not, and trying to agree on what happened. And every church disagrees slightly with what they will include in what they call the New Testament, and that must mean something, too. If it was really the word of the Lord, wouldn't it be something we'd all agree on? Even the Bible that I was taught as a girl didn't claim there was only one God; it just said there was only one we were allowed to follow as the Almighty. I read in one of my magazines about that Socrates. Well, people wrote about him after he died, just like they did Jesus, but nobody goes around worshiping him, do they? They killed him, too, for what he thought, just like Jesus, but they gave him a poison drink and he just fell asleep. That feels like a much more humane thing to do than beating a man senseless and hanging him on a cross, doesn't it?

CHAPTER 41

The things that are growing in the world now, and the birds notice all of them, are terrifying me because people are starting to say that their God is the only one, and the birds are all saying to each other that this is going to be the downfall of the world. All of them Bible-beaters are ready for it all to end, though! One of these days, enough of them are going to be in power that they will bring the end on, and since I won't be here I don't really care. But I don't want the world to be messed up for the birds. They don't deserve that. They have been here for millions of years before us and they should be allowed to stay millions of years after.

I think the Catholics that have surrounded me my whole life are just simpletons. They want it all to be explained away with a few stories. I just have to believe that we are immortal, that we keep coming back and learning from our forever days. If we don't, what is the learning for? Everything alive must be related, and the birds are sure proof of that. They have lives every bit as complex as ours; we just don't notice them. But they notice us. They spy on everything we do. Then they forget it. Think what they could do if they could remember us, but they have no memory at all except for their most basic needs. It is us, the mere mortals, who keep memories alive and keep ourselves stuck on forever days because we can't let them die.

I am so limited by what I can actually see with my own two eyes, which isn't much. Birds can't see what is right in front of them, and they move so fast when they are flying that it must all be such a blur to them.

They put the blurred sights together with their memories, and they see all the waves that are in the air now, things we hear but cannot see. Yet they somehow manage to find their way to Mexico or farther every winter, and come back to my yard the next year. I can just hear you asking how I know it is the same birds returning. Well, they are the same. There are some things you just know.

CHAPTER 42

I loved working at the telephone office for all of those years because of everything I heard—just like the birds sitting on the lines, listening but never telling. I never forgot things I learned from overhearing phone conversations. There was not a single case of adultery or a family squabble in all of Ophelia that I didn't know about then, but I wouldn't even tell Slick about them. I was quite happy keeping all that to myself. And I talked to my sisters almost every day, anytime I had a free second at the phone office, which happened a lot. I'd sit on the phone desk at home in our dining room for hours, but I never once told any of them about the drunks they lived next door to, or the lowlifes who beat up their wives and kids and they just never knew it. Every time they heard an ambulance, they would call me at the telephone office to see what it was. I never told them, not once, even though I knew. And I'd see all of them people I knew all about at the grocery store or the Dog and Suds, and anything I knew about them that no one else could possibly know made me feel safe. Knowing things is like sugar: you can never have too much, but it doesn't mean you have to do anything with what you know.

From the telephone office I could tell what people was really like. In person, people can fool you. They can smile all the time, and that dupes a lot of folks. I'm not that impressed with people who have a beautiful smile. Most often people are lost in thoughts or worries, and I always think if they are smiling it is for my benefit, because they have noticed me there, and I always trust that. If people were smiling when they didn't know anyone was looking at them, then I found that incredibly beautiful. After I retired from the phone office, I found it harder to get to know people. At least I did until my forever day.

CHAPTER 43

All of my sisters were born in the last century, before we started the oughts, can you imagine? I'm the only twentieth-century girl in my family, and even that was just under the wire. Edith, Lucy, Rachel, and Madge were all before me. The five Borders girls. Weren't we a sight? Now they have all passed on, and I haven't been able to find a thing about them here. I ask and ask, and I'm told they are all stuck in their own forever days, refusing to move on, and I can't see them until they do. They say this to me as some kind of lesson with a little bit of warning hidden in it, but I haven't figured it out yet.

We moved to Ophelia after I was born, not long after they moved the Richmond–Evansville train, and without that train there would be no way for Daddy to get work, no way to get anywhere. I didn't think there could be anything sadder than an abandoned train line. They didn't take the tracks away; they just stopped using them. Mama and I went up there shortly after the war, the first war, which was about twenty years after the trains stopped rolling, and I could hardly believe it. You could tell it had been there but nature had already taken it back. My memories flit around now: the birds were never right during the second war. You can't have an entire world trying to kill each other and not expect the birds to feel it. The thing is, they feel things before we do. They know what is going to happen to the world well before we do because they know how to listen to the world. Birds don't listen to small things like opinions.

CHAPTER 44

The only social thing I did regular was go to Bingo on Thursday nights at the K of C. I loved the game, and loved to gamble in general, though for some reason Catholics never seemed to view Bingo as gambling. I guess the money they made from it was just as green as the money the people gave on Sundays, and the Catholics always knew how to rake in the money. I could arrive just before it started without all the small talk, and because of the way the game is played, I also didn't have to talk to anybody during it. Almost every lady in town had a card club of some kind, many of them had more than one, but I couldn't stand the thought of having to talk and gossip with those ladies every week. They all knew that I'd worked in the phone office and I knew everything about everybody, and I didn't want to be grilled for information. Even after I retired from the telephone office, I could trace every bit of gossip from all over town from a specific card club or another. They were like little tribes and though they didn't notice it, some of them was mean. Most of the clubs stayed together for forty-five to fifty years, and when a lady died she would be replaced by someone identified long before. There was no way in if you wasn't already there.

CHAPTER 45

I'm not sure who these people are. They keep telling me but I forget. The notes they send me tell more and more, but I don't believe them. Today they sent me one that said Slick would drive forty miles at 4:00 a.m. to St. Meinrad so he could listen to the monks sing at dawn, then drive back to Ophelia to open the station. I can't begin to believe that. Slick would get up early and try to get the station open as early as he could. I know sometimes he would eat breakfast at the Arrow so as not to wake me if I was asleep on the couch, but that doesn't mean he would be gone for two to three hours before the station got open. The Arrow never opened before 6:00. If he'd been going to St. Meinrad all those years, he could have gotten up to all kinds of trouble. The note today said something about singing, but who would have driven all that way just to hear some singing? But Lordy, he did have some strange ways about him, so maybe he did.

I sure didn't want to stir up more snakes than I could kill, and I wasn't sure what to do. A man is going to have his stirrings, isn't he? And I knew that I'd not been able to give Slick the right outlet for his longings. I did try, and I hope that trying must count for something here, but I just could never quite get there. As long as I could tell him I loved him and make him feel safe and looked after, I felt I was doing my wifely duty, but of course I knew I wasn't, not really. That's what all these notes are trying to get at, I know. They want me to see all of it as though I wasn't there.

Snakes. I just mentioned snakes, and I hate snakes more than I hate anything. I think some smart character should go all around the world and kill every single snake and wipe them off the face of the earth. Why do we need them? What earthly good do they do? I'm no Bible-beater, but that book sure got the snakes right. They can swallow something larger than they are! What on earth? Mama told me about one that ate a whole calf when she was a girl. I read that snakes are dinosaurs that didn't get killed off. Why not? Of course, the birds are dinosaurs, too, but they are different. Snakes are stupid and birds are brilliant. I keep a little charm of St. Patrick on my dressing table because he's the one who made all the snakes leave Ireland. Where is our St. Patrick now?

CHAPTER 46

Ginger was our golden retriever and a good birder if she wanted to be, though she wouldn't ever harm birds. She just liked to stir them up just so's they'd come say hello to me. I named her after my favorite actress, Ginger Rogers. By the time we got Ginger in Odon in the early '60s, I knew most of the groundlings in our area by name and they knew me, trusted me. Our yard was big, especially for a city lot, and it surprised me that over time Ginger learned which birds to chase away and which to let stay, and the birds seemed to understand it, too. Ginger and I almost had the same mind. She was the only dog I ever felt that for. Ginger looked me right in the eye, and I was the only other being on earth she did that to. Not Slick, not any other person. Ginger and I could really hear each other, and you just don't see that very often. I knew Ginger knew that I could hear the birds like she did.

Ginger loved Hershey bars. All of my nieces and nephews for years would repeat what they'd learned at school or from their parents, that chocolate was poison to dogs. I'd always tell them, "Well, somebody forgot to tell that to Ginger, because she loves them Hershey bars and sometimes I give her Oreos, too, if I'm out of the Hersheys, and she's as healthy as a g.d. horse!" I finally had to resort to almost cursing, since they mentioned it so often. Ginger lived almost eighteen years, so I guess the chocolate didn't kill her, now, did it? You've never seen anybody love anything more than she loved them Hershey bars.

Ginger had the run of the house, but her real territory was the basement. We had a sump pump down there in the room off the coal furnace. Most of the houses in Ophelia replaced their coal furnaces over time, but we never did. I didn't want the expense and the mess of taking the coal out of there, and, anyway, coal gave off good heat and it was cheap to find. The family thought we lived too old-fashioned, because I also collected rainwater in the same rain barrel that was at the house when we bought it, and I still used the well water for the birds and the gardening, even after we hooked up to the city plumbing. Everybody else had long plugged up their wells, but I liked not having to pay for water for the birds. The well stayed full and I liked to pump it out like I did when I was girl.

The family also talked behind our backs, never right to my face, about Ginger going to the bathroom in our basement. But I couldn't take her outside at all times of the year. Sometimes it was too cold or it would be raining or snowing. And I have access to a bathroom whenever I want to go, so she should, too. I put newspapers down for her and she always used them. Ginger was never one to have accidents upstairs. She would go downstairs, and I always kept it very clean so you couldn't smell it.

Nighttime cars in little towns create the most terrible silent shadows a few seconds before you hear their motors. You can never be quite sure how far away the car is, or even if it is a car. Sometimes people coming out of their houses or working in garages can create the shadows, too, and that's why I usually avoided being outside at night. That's one of the reasons I put papers down for Ginger in the basement, so we wouldn't always have to go out in the shadows. Even though the train engines upset the birds and rattled the floorboards of every house, at least you knew what they were. It was the nighttime shadows that you had to watch out for, and they always scared me.

CHAPTER 47

I was invisible to most people because I made myself that way. I wanted to blend into the background, not be noticed, because the people who were noticed had to carry that with them and be noticed more the next time. The price of being noticed was just too high. I didn't want people to remember me. There were things that made me happy and made me feel alive, and all I wanted was more of those things; I wanted to hold on to them, and I knew I couldn't if people was noticing me all the time. But the world kept moving so much, kept growing, kept changing. I couldn't keep up, and, truth be told, I didn't want to keep up. I loved our little house, all of our collecting, my dolls, Ginger, and the nieces and nephews when they were little. I didn't need for any of it to change. I've met people here who were so wise about change. They even seemed to want everything to change so they could "experience" more. I was happy to keep doing what we were doing. I didn't need anything new or "more." I loved what I had. Isn't being content with what you have one of the signs of living right?

I bought all kinds of new dresses for my dolls earlier that year, in all of the after-Christmas sales. I hadn't really changed them for ten or twelve years. How the time flies! I kept them all in Mama's room so I could go in there whenever I wanted and dress them, talk to them, whatever I felt like. The family was all talking about my dolls by the time of my forever day, but that was mostly because Stevie was making fun of them and telling everyone that I sometimes put a doll at the kitchen table to eat with us. That deadbeat mom of his made sure everybody heard about that. Slick and I never had children of our own so I don't see anything wrong with putting one of my dolls at the table. I just loved those dolls, especially the one I found at Block's in Indianapolis in the early '60s. She was named Susie and she could walk if you put her arm in a certain position. She was about the size of a three-year-old so it was easy to find pretty dresses for her. There weren't harm in playing with dolls when I was a little girl, and I don't reckon there was any harm later, either, but you'd sure have thought there was by the way the family talked about it.

I found ruffs in the front yard the autumn before, as the leaves turned in October of '72, which I never did understand. How did they lose their way and stray so far from the water? The other birds were so upset by the ruffs being there, even though they didn't stay long, that I wasn't sure if we weren't in for a full-scale bird rebellion. There are creatures that just can't get along, but the ruffs being there had to mean something. They had a birdsong unlike any I'd ever heard before. And where did they go from Indiana? It felt like some kind of omen, a warning not to stray too far from myself. I hated seeing the robins so upset, since they was normally the most friendly of the yard birds. Since Ginger was still with us on that 1973 forever day, she was always with me when I was in the yard, and the robins weren't the least bit upset by her. All the other birds would *shreep* and flee the yard the moment Ginger came outside, even though I never once saw her chase any bird. I could leave her off the leash at any time of day and she would just stay right with me. Birds knew that Ginger didn't mean them no harm; she'd just chase smells around the yard that didn't seem to have anything to do with them.

Their songs changed whenever a cat came around the yard, though. I hated every single one of our neighbor cats because they hunted the birds and preyed on the weaker ones, and then didn't even bother to eat them after they killed them. I can't stand any animal that hunts the weak. If the dangers were something larger, like if a tornado was coming or even just a bad thunderstorm, the birdsong totally changed. I could tell that the birds were reacting, but up till that time I still couldn't tell exactly what they were saying to each other, sort of like when I watched Chinese movies at midnight from that weird station in Indianapolis, on the winter nights when the signal reached far enough south. I could never understand a word they said but I knew they was saying something.

CHAPTER 48

Our little house used to be the second floor of the house next door. We watched them cut it off and move it, spring of '32. It was hard to believe that it would be cheaper than just building a new house, but in those days it was. The house next door was way too big for what they needed, so we built a basement, sump pump, and fireplace and had them place the second floor of their house on our foundation, like a boy playing with Lincoln Logs. It was very small but it was the amount of space we needed and could afford. We'd planned to build a nice house a few years later, with a plan I loved from the Sears catalog, on the new highway, but then the Japs bombed Pearl Harbor and we had to wait until after the war.

And you know what happened then? The g.d. Catholic Church bought all the land around there and planned to build a gym and high school. They bought the land from under us, and didn't even give us a chance to bid. It all happened during the war and we just did not have the money to fight it, but if Slick had been home and working, we'd have kept that school from being built. That school didn't last more than twenty years, anyway, because their old building burned down and they had to consolidate with the public school, like they should have done from the start. I was so mad at them for keeping us from building our dream home. I kept the blueprints in the dining room hutch, always hoping we could build it somewhere else, but of course we never did. I take them out every few years or so and look at what we might have had. It seems strange to me now that I saved them, because it always makes me sad to look at them.

But I liked to look at maps, too, much more than I liked to travel, so maybe that was just how I was.

Our house had a little attic and I'm sure I've put a few things up there, but I can't anymore remember what. I've sometimes heard noises from up there, even a voice or two, and usually I'm scared of things like that, but these voices haven't scared me. They aren't the voices of bad people, and they don't sound like the birds, neither. They seem to be protecting me and protecting Ginger.

I tried to change the birdbaths and bird feeders out in the yard every day. The bird feeders Slick built for me that I could clean and change from indoors were the great joy of our little house. When we first moved in, chopped off from the house next door, there was a big front porch that we didn't use; it was just a cheap feature to build. It was the style in those days that people would take walks in the early morning and early evening, and if you had a big front porch like we did, everybody who was walking would stop by and talk. I couldn't stand to be around all those people and think about what to say to them every night; same reason I couldn't ever stand to go to church. Because before and after church you had to make small talk about what you were cooking and what you were doing for holidays, and everybody's ills. Oh, I can't stand to do that. I'd so much rather be inside watching one of my shows or cooking something for the nieces and nephews.

So we enclosed the front porch, which gave us great big windows on three sides and an entirely new front door, which I felt we needed because before the war I once found a traveling salesman who'd been standing there staring at me for God knows how long. I knew right then and there that we were going to put in a solid door instead of the glass and blinds that were so popular then. From the other windows, you couldn't see into the house, because the front door covered the only door into the living room. My arrangement worked, and I never had another traveling salesman staring at me. And the new front to the house had so many windows that it felt like another room altogether, and a greenhouse at that. Outside every new window, eight of them at first, Slick built me a bird feeder, all I had to do was open up the window and change the seed or the hummingbird sugar water. Oh, how I loved those feeders, because I could sit there for hours and watch them birds. I always felt, even from when I was a little girl, that the birds were trying to tell me something. By my forever day, in 1973, I was absolutely sure the birds were not only talking directly to me but trying desperately to warn me of something growing in the world. Why they chose me, I'll never know. There was a layer between us that I knew I would be able to get through before too much longer.

You see, it wasn't that I could understand their birdsong; that would be impossible. But there was other ways they tried to talk to me. Birds can see things we can't. That won't be much of a surprise to people, I guess. But all the things we hear, the things that travel through the air invisible to us, they can see. Like radio waves: we hear them when we are tuned in to the right frequency, but the birds can see them all the time. And I think that over time the sight of the waves has changed the birds. I say this because of something that happened just after my forever day, and I know I'm right about this. Birds can see the radio signals, but that's not *all* they see. And it shows up to them as straight lines that pulse across their eyes, right across anything they are looking at. Their sight can get very confused by things we can't see at all. And despite all those distractions, the birds can still find their food, find their feeders at my windows, and manage to notice us when we come into the yard.

CHAPTER 49

The winter before my forever day, Slick decided we should take a road trip somewhere.

"Oh my Lord, Slick," I told him, "all that is on the TV set is how there's an oil shortage and nobody will be able to go anywhere."

"I've got oil stored up in the northern part of the county, so we will be fine."

It dawned on me. "What do you mean you have oil stored up in the county? What on earth?"

"That monsignor who comes around sometimes from St. Meinrad, you remember him? For the last year he's been paying me to send one of our supply trucks each week up to a storage facility they have up on a farm someplace," Slick said.

"And you've been doing it? Why didn't you tell me?" I said, feeling we were in deep shit. I hated when other people used that word, but I didn't mind it for myself when it was the right word, which it sure was in this case.

"It's fine, Birdie. He's high up in the church," Slick said.

"How can you be so stupid? You can't just stockpile oil when there is an energy crisis. What is he using it for?"

"I don't rightly know. But I guess they use it for the church, to be sure they don't run out of oil right now," Slick said.

"And we are supposed to keep our houses at sixty-eight degrees! Can you imagine? We are all catching our deaths of cold while that church is probably selling oil illegally and using you as a scapegoat!"

"Sixty-eight is good sleeping weather, Birdie-wordy."

"Who owns this storage up in the north part of the county? We sure aren't taking a road trip, except maybe up there to see what the heck is going on," I screamed at him. I was so angry that he'd put us in danger.

"We are fine, Birdie. You mustn't upset yourself. We can take a trip."

"If we drive east and run out of gas, what good is it to have oil stored up in Martin County?"

"Well, I didn't think all the way through that. But we can buy oil on the road. I just mean we will have plenty when we get back."

"Have you been able to use any of this oil that you've delivered to the Catholics? Who owns this storage?"

"Well, I haven't needed it. It is owned by a guy named Daniel."

I searched my memory. It had been a few years since I'd worked at the phone office, but I knew no one in the county named Daniel. And I knew we had to get up there to see what was going on. I wanted to see these oil storage tanks. Something was fishy about all of it. I made Slick drive us right up there the next day.

I hadn't been up in the north part of the county for years. Hadn't had call to. It was all familiar to me from childhood, but so much was gone or just left to rot. I was happy to see some of the things. We went through the seven curves of little Dover Hill, and all I could think about was the wonderful times we used to have up there at the general store with my niece Sue, when she and her husband owned it. Dover Hill used to feel so alive and filled with people, but by '73 there was almost nothing left. Home after home abandoned. The hotel turned into a big house. The general store just used for storage for something.

There was barely anything to Sun Creek anymore, either, but it used to run like the dickens when I was a kid. We drove over to McBride's Bluff just so I could see it again. Kids have spray-painted horrible things all over it, and it is just ruined. We drove up to Indian Springs where I was born, but it is all gone now. Not one thing left from my childhood.

Hard to believe, isn't it? A town that used to be thriving is now just gone. Given back to nature. We went on up through Williams, which has never been the same since they put up the dam. I know they probably needed it, but I think it just ruined the place. All the big promises of the dam bringing jobs, all the things politicians say. I guess the dam prevents flooding, that's what they say at least, and Ophelia hasn't flooded in years so maybe they were right.

We pulled up into a road north of Williams, headed for wherever this place was, and I noticed the birds sending us all kinds of warnings, not just the tree-line birds but the groundlings, too. And I remembered something about some kind of commune going into the north part of the county just a few years before. I heard some of them talking about it over the phone lines, but it was harder to listen in during my last few years, so things were more difficult to know. They was a bunch of those 1960s hippies, not a bit different from the gypsies fifty years before, if you ask me. The birds were trying to tell us to stay away but I sure had to see all this oil to believe it.

I saw a gun tower, just like we was pulling into a prison. There wasn't anybody up in it just then, but there it was, as sure as you're born, something I never thought I'd see: a gun tower in Martin County. Papa would not have known what to think.

"Slick, I have a bad feeling about all of this. I think we should turn around," I said, not really wanting to turn around.

"We'll be just fine. I know it can't be much farther up here."

We came to a gate. I knew this countryside, so I knew we weren't over at the naval weapons depot that took up most of northern Martin County. We were east of there, and there shouldn't be anything that looked like this gate.

"Slick, this is that commune—all those hippies who live together."

"Pajama-something?"

"Good God. What have you gotten us mixed up in?" I was furious at that man.

"That monsignor is the one mixed up in it, not us."

"You've been delivering trucks of oil up here, Slick!"

"Well, the monsignor has been paying for it. It's not like I've done it for charity."

"Who else knows about this?"

"I don't know. I never thought it was any kind of big deal until you started carrying on," Slick said. He always did make light of things that were serious.

Just as I was about to make us turn around, the gate opened, even though there was nobody around to see us. I was petrified and said so, but Slick pulled us into that gate and it didn't matter one bit what I said. The gate closed behind us and I was sure these would be my last moments on earth. We drove for some time up through a valley, and all of a sudden we were in a little village, bigger than Indian Springs had ever been. There was a huge lumber mill. A couple of men came out to greet us.

"Peace to you both. How can we help you?" one of the boys said.

"Is there a Daniel here?" I said before Slick could get his thoughts together.

"Of course, ma'am. Would you like to talk to Daniel?" The boys were very polite.

"Yes, we would," I said. Slick said not a thing, even when I hit his arm to get him to talk.

And lickety-split, there he was at our car window.

"Welcome to Padanaram, good friends," Daniel said. "What can I do for you?"

Slick answered, "I've been sending my oil supplier up here for a while, as the monsignor asked me to do. We thought we'd drive up to see it."

"You must be Slick! You want to see the oil storage?" Daniel asked.

"If you don't mind," Slick said.

"I'm afraid I don't have access to it, Slick. I'm sorry."

"Why on earth not?" I asked.

"Well, all of this land belongs to the Catholic Church. We are on a long-term lease from them, but they have a section of the land over by the naval depot that is not accessible to us, or anyone. Would you like to look at our home, see our dining area?"

Something just didn't feel right about all of this, but I had to admit that Daniel was nice enough. So, we parked and went up to their big building. Everything was made of the most beautiful wood you ever saw, like the Amish homes, only they had electricity. They showed us their big dining area.

"Everyone eats every meal together here. We share everything," Daniel said. "No one goes hungry."

"Is this a commune?" Slick asked. I shot him such a look.

"Yes, Slick. It is a commune. But we aren't like the hippies you've read about. We are respectful of each other. We are a very religious community. We believe in the redemption of Jesus Christ. Do you?"

I was taken aback to be asked such a direct question about my private views. I was embarrassed and didn't know what to say, so I asked him what their name meant.

"Our name means 'the field of Aram' from the Aramaic language, God's language—so we like to feel we are in God's valley."

CHAPTER 50

It was all more than I could understand. They seemed to not have much privacy, but there were several hundred people living there together, so it must have been what they wanted. I sure wouldn't do it. Did they all sleep together or trade wives or something? I didn't dare ask. Slick wanted to see the lumber mill so Daniel took us over there. It was a huge operation.

"You must make a pretty penny from all this," Slick said, looking over the lumber mill.

"It is very lucrative, Slick. And we pour every cent we make back into our community. We grow a lot of our food here and many of our people work in those gardens, but we also drive to Bedford to buy what we need. We aren't afraid of cars or technology. We just reject the accepted capitalist view of things, that you work and others make the money."

I didn't rightly know what he meant. I mean, capitalism is just what the country is, right? I couldn't understand how you could still live in a country but not be a part of it. It had made me so mad when the Amish didn't go fight for their country.

"Can people leave here if they want? You've got gun towers up at the gate." I couldn't quite believe I had the nerve to ask him that, but Daniel was good at making us feel comfortable.

"Everyone is here voluntarily. No one is forced to stay. And that isn't a gun tower. It's for watching out for forest fires. It belongs to the county, and rangers will be up there on high-danger days and nights. We always take them food and drink when they are on watch. They are, after all, protecting all of us."

Well, Daniel had an answer for everything, so before we left I got up the gumption to ask him about the bedrooms.

"No, ma'am. Despite all the gossip about us, we don't wife swap. Couples come here and stay together as a family, which we encourage because we feel that is part of God's plan for the world. Now, couples have their issues here, just like anywhere, but this is a collective community. We share our worldly goods but not our heaven-sent bodies."

Well, that was that. We drove back to Ophelia almost in silence, as there wasn't much to say about what we saw. The oil, though, that was a real worry. Something strange was going on with the church and I had to get to the bottom of that.

CHAPTER 51

We never had places to eat in Ophelia, not to speak of, except maybe the Dairy Master, which did make a mean breaded tenderloin and sometimes there was nothing better. But we didn't eat those much because we liked to drive to the larger neighbor towns to eat dinner. We weren't ever ones to go to a place with tablecloths, not that there were many of those; we liked the diners and drive-ins.

After the war, they opened the nicest restaurant Ophelia ever had, the Arrow Café, and we did like to have that in town. It closed, like everything good, after Watergate. Well, I don't know if Richard Nixon had anything to do with that, but the whole country did seem to go to pot with him. It is still amazing what was taken away from the world in those years around my forever day. The Arrow was right next to our station so Slick saw every person who went in and out of there. They had a café counter, and during the day they had a soda fountain that would draw all the boys from the Catholic school to buy pretzels and snacks after school. Them boys always seemed to have money to spend, and they would stop in the station, too. A lot of them was looking for a man to talk to, you know? So they went to Slick, and of course he never met a stranger. All they ever wanted to talk about was the priests. Those boys talked about them priests like they were the gods instead of just another man with all of a man's problems and pulls. I never trusted any priest. They were like an army all dressed in black. Slick came home in those years full of stories about the boys, and it felt to me like he was just a tick too full of fascination for the priests. I wasn't fully sure what it meant then.

On Fridays we would have time to run to Washington to buy groceries and have supper somewhere and still be back for the 8:00 programs Jenny liked so much. Sometimes we'd even have time to go by their beautiful park, where there were so many birds—a lot more than we had in Ophelia. I'd buy them a dozen loaves of the cheapest bread and feed it to them. Sometimes we'd go to Helphenstine's where they'd carhop you, and their burgers were just a dream come true, if we didn't go to the White Steamer. Those were our favorite places in Washington, and Jenny loved them both, too. I swear that little girl might just turn into a hamburger one of these days, and I couldn't ever get her to eat anything else, not until she grew up.

On Fridays we could get back in time for *The Brady Bunch* and *The Partridge Family* at 8:00, take a little break for milk and cookies at 9:00 because there was nothing on that any of us liked, then *The Odd Couple* at 9:30, which was my absolute favorite show ever to be on television, and always that *Love, American Style*, which was way too racy for Jenny so I usually put her to bed when it started and I usually let Slick watch it alone since it was so dirty. I didn't like that kind of a show.

Just before my forever day was the night we took Stevie with us, along with little Jenny. It had to be a Saturday, because I absolutely remember being back for *The Paul Lynde Show* at 8:30, so we must have gone somewhere a little farther away like Vincennes. I loved Paul Lynde and I still can't believe that stupid network took his show off the air so fast. Look at some of the stuff they left on! And that year, Saturday night from 9:00 to 11:00 was absolutely golden, a forever time if there ever was one: Mary Tyler Moore, Bob Newhart, and Carol Burnett all back to back. I let Stevie and Jenny watch all the way to the end of Carol Burnett but then I made them both go to bed. It was a particularly cold winter that year, which made me especially blue because we had fewer winter birds. The hardy ones, though, needed more food and they ate like dinosaurs that year.

CHAPTER 52

Strange that for years it was always us townsfolk who noticed the birds. Heck, it was always us who noticed *anything* about nature. Birds don't even know they can fly because they've never known anything else. They can't see their wings. Music and movies were just pretty things that man created, and I liked them enough, but I could have lived without them if I really had to. The happiest things in my life were trees and birds, and they are the two creations of God that make life beautiful.

That wasn't true for the farmers, especially the Amish. It seems to me they all hated anything in nature because it interfered with their daily work. Nature was just a hindrance to them, like the river, just a thing that was in the way of the other side. I'd seen them out there on their tractors, if they were modern farmers, and on their horses, if they were Amish, sometimes field to field waving to each other, right on the edge of the river. An entire world of beauty was floating by them and they wouldn't even notice it, and not just beauty, but history. The river told you everything if you knew how to listen to it, just like the birds did. The birds would dive and pick over their fields, ready to tell the farmers all sorts of things about the land and the weather, yet all they ever seemed to be able to do was shoot at them for it.

I only ever met one farmer who listened to the birds, and she moved away to Chicago or someplace, as they all tended to do. Trees weren't beautiful to a farmer because they threw shade all over their garden in summer, and any part of their fields that was shaded meant trees got ripped down, which always just broke my heart. When I got potato bugs in our larder out back, I sat and looked in wonder at how beautiful they were, with their hard backs that looked like someone had painted them each specially; no two were alike. But out on the farms, they would throw those beautiful things into an open fire and burn them alive.

I didn't like bats. I never really thought of bats as birds, even though they fly. Hawks can kill bats, though, so birds really are the rulers of the sky. Crows and jays are so smart that they will land on ant colonies and let the ants clean them up. I first saw it down by the House Rock when I was a girl, and I still think it is one of the most amazing facts of life, and everybody thought Tom Sawyer was so smart for getting his friends to whitewash the fence! That kid had nothing on the birds.

CHAPTER 53

But even in town we had to deal with people who thought nature was just one more enemy. November of '63 we had especially heavy migrations of birds all around Ophelia, especially ducks, and the hunters were out in armies that month. I would see them come into town from my vantage point at the telephone office.

I miss that building in downtown Ophelia. They tore it down in the '70s, like they did everything good. It was the nicest old building, too, with a billing office on the street, maintenance storage behind it, and the telephone exchange upstairs alongside a sweet apartment that they rented out.

I could see everything that went on in town from up there, and I saw them hunters come into town, probably to go to the Arrow on their break from shooting birds. The birds knew what they were up to, and the highest type of birds got the hell out of their way but quick. Of course the birds who were younger in their life cycle didn't know enough to get out of the way. I eventually got to where I could tell them and they would listen, but that was only near my forever day ten years later. I couldn't talk to them yet in '63.

I'm always surprised at what people don't believe, as though the things that you know are subject to believing. If they think about it at all, they know that birds are old, which they are. They are living dinosaurs, but that doesn't mean their souls are all the same age. I figure that it is the same with people, because why would it be any different? But you'd never find me saying that over there. Those churches would go crazy with that idea, even just with the idea that birds know things. To think that our souls are elastic, and that they last, they will go that far. But they can't, or won't, cope with anything that doesn't have to do with how they think of God. They think God created everything at the same time, some of them even think that dinosaurs and people lived at the same time. Now, where does that leave the birds? But I grew up around these people, and some of them had more schooling than me and they still believed that nonsense. Still, you can't judge people by what they think, only by what they do.

CHAPTER 54

Though a lot of the nieces and nephews through the years kept trying to convince me, I never wanted a parrot. I could understand the real language of the birds, so I sure didn't need a bird that just aped me talking. That would be like living with a talking telephone. Parrots are mimics, which is a beautiful thing, since most people are mimics, too, but they can't put into words what they really see. They can only do that with other birds and with diviners like me.

Starlings, finches, and sparrows were my favorite birds because I think they needed me the most. It is a wonderful thing to feel needed. After my last forever day, they needed me all the more. Slick did, too. I started going to East Side Park every morning after breakfast. I would buy the cheapest loaves of bread I could find, sometimes buying a dozen or so, and then I'd buy all the old bread that was marked down, and drive out to the park and feed it to the birds. I loved how the birds depended on me.

CHAPTER 55

About ten years into the business, Slick was able to buy a tow truck, one of only two in a twenty-five-mile radius, but I didn't like it because the back of it was a cross and one of Slick's workers, some young smart aleck, painted the crucified Jesus across it. So many people around town thought it was "beautiful" to have this reminder as their car was being hitched to a truck, but I thought it blasphemous and vulgar. I kept mother's crucifixes all through the house, particularly the one on top of the piano that she especially loved. I even bought the blond Baldwin because it matched the wood on that little cross. Now, I know I was not a churchgoing Christian, but there are things one does not ever joke about, and the crucifixion is one of those. Putting that on a tow truck! But Slick left it there for years, not wanting to upset the boys who worked for him who thought it was so meaningful. I know they didn't mean it as a joke, but when other people saw it they took it as funny. I saw people around town pointing to it and laughing. More fake Christians.

When I was a little girl, I used to think the moon died every night. For me everything about nighttime was told by the birds, so when they got quiet at night I used to think they died, too. It was a long time before I realized that moonless nights didn't mean things always died. I came to know that there was a lot of life at night. I'm noticing that the sky here seems to know me just like it used to back in Ophelia when I was little. That sky knew every tree and bird, and it knew me, too. There are birds here, even some that I used to know and haven't seen in so long, and they know a little more about me each hour.

They've asked me what frightens me about moving on from my forever day. I guess I worry most about forgetting the things that I am trying desperately to remember. Already the littlest things from many years ago are gone, just erased from my mind. I used to be able to remember the smallest things, the smell and feel of things, but so much of that is gone. There was a certain smell to houses before air conditioning, before the second war. Every once in a while, I would wander into the scent again when I visited some of the older folks, and the few times I was ever in an Amish house, there it was.

CHAPTER 56

Nearly everybody in Ophelia had an Amish lady as housekeeper. They came into town on buggies that they parked at the square, and we would all trade carpooling them around town. Our house was so small it only took half a day, but of course the doctors and bankers had big houses where the Amish ladies worked two or three days a week. Those ladies knew absolutely everything about all of us, which is why I never let Sylvia be in the house alone. I didn't want her to ever see those dirty salt and pepper shakers, or every single person in Amish-land would know about it that very night.

I will say this for Sylvia and all those girls: they did not gossip with townsfolk, for whatever they said to each other on the buggy rides home. I can honestly say I loved Sylvia, and I didn't have many outside my family I could say that about. She was such a wonderful God-loving woman. She was funny, and she loved a good story, but she was never mean. She was devoted to every household she worked for, and her ironing and cleaning was the finest you'd ever find. She was afraid of dogs, so I had to pen Ginger up downstairs when she was in the house, but that also helped because I didn't have to show Sylvia the part of the basement where Ginger went potty. I know she would have tried to clean it up, and I gave up on keeping that part of the basement clean years ago. It was near the sump pump, and I just didn't think the smell mattered much. You couldn't smell it upstairs, anyway.

CHAPTER 57

I never much liked to drive out to Amish country because the farm smells were so strong, but I did love seeing and hearing so many birds out there so free and safe. In truth, it wasn't the smells that kept me from Amish country. When I was little, before the Pinnacle, we went out to an Amish funeral of somebody Mama knew. We were the only ones there who weren't Amish, and that alone would have made me feel uneasy, but there was a lot more.

They had spread straw all over their lane so the horses' hooves would be quiet. When we went in the house, there was people sitting on benches all over the place, all dressed in black just staring forward, silent. Their usual white curtains were draped with black bunting. They took us into a little room off to the left and closed the door behind us. Suddenly we were in a room with a pine coffin propped up on both ends by two simple chairs. There was nothing else in the room but a candle. They lifted the lid off the coffin and latched it open at the top with a little hook. There was a man inside. Nobody was crying or saying a word. Mama was praying, and I knew I was supposed to be, but I couldn't. All I could do was listen to the birds outside who were trying to help someone. The man in coffin was dead but the birds were saying it wasn't his time. And when a person leaves life before their time, the birds still see them as if they were alive. They stay in and around their life, stuck in a forever time, unable to move on until their passing arrives. There is no escaping the truth of this. People who think they can take their own life are fooling themselves, because while you might be dead to the people who knew you, you're not dead to the birds or to any of the creatures who can see truths.

CHAPTER 58

Gene Stratton-Porter was my childhood hero. How I loved her books, each one of which I checked out a million times from the Ophelia library. I first got to know her from reading her columns in *Good House-keeping*. She was an Indiana girl, and I always felt connected to her that way, but it was more because she understood the land and how it needed to be preserved for the birds. We went to visit her Cabin at Wildflower Woods years ago, way up north around Rome City. If only I'd had her mind and her gumption. She had the nerve to move to California right after the first war, even though she was no youngster then, and she kept on writing books that I just loved. She spoke right to me. I must have read *A Girl of the Limberlost* a thousand times, and I kept it within eyesight all my life. She was against using bird feathers in hats, and I always loved that she went to bat for the birds. When I was seven, my Christmas gift was her book, *What I Have Done With Birds*. She wrote in a way that I could understand, which I always appreciated since I loved to read, but so many writers wrote in a way I just couldn't understand.

I read all day, every day, when I was at the telephone office, especially in those wonderful early years when I was there by myself. There would be periods when it was really busy, like the first hour of business in the morning, or anytime around somebody's death. But there were long periods when I didn't have much to do, and I would read. I read every magazine, and I loved them all so much that I couldn't bear to part with them. So I set up shelves in the basement, and it was there that I stored every magazine I ever bought or subscribed to. I know the family thought it was crazy that I saved them all. But I did go back and read them from time to time, and I did love them. Gratitude for one's collections is the key to life, I now know.

CHAPTER 59

After the second war, the first big purchase Slick and I made was the blond upright piano we found in Vincennes in the 1950s. I loved it like it was alive. We had only one place in the whole house where it could fit but it looked just perfect there, right in the corner of the living room. That piano cost us more than any car we ever bought, about three thousand dollars—the most expensive thing we owned—and it sat in a house that had cost just a little more than that twenty-five years before.

I put a little Magnus Chord Organ next to it that I got in the late '50s, and it made the music a little easier for me because you only had to push one button with your left hand to play a chord. I bought a ton of sheet music, all my favorite songs, and I intended to play every one. But all my life I had to write the notes in, and when the songs had lots of sharps and flats, like "Stardust," by the time you read all the note names you might as well have just spent the time learning to read music, but my mind could just never grasp it. I never stopped going to the piano whenever the house was empty and trying my best to play some of my favorite songs. And in the years after the war, Vincennes had three music stores, Washington had two, and between them I could find a lot of great sheet music. I waited for the sheet music releases like most people waited for records. By my forever day I had several thousand pieces of sheet music, all stacked by the piano in an old mail sorter we got from Slick's brother.

CHAPTER 60

I bought a lot of records, too, as I loved to listen to them on our stereos in the front porch room. We had two stereos because I didn't want to give up my collection of 78s, and our newer one played 33s and 45s. I couldn't afford the ones that played all three kinds of records. I would sit out there for hours listening to hymns on my old 78s, or to that Jo Ann Castle. I know I had every record she ever made. I wanted to play like that girl! Her fingers moved so fast you'd think she'd take off and fly, and she always looked like she was having so much fun. Usually when you saw piano players on television they looked so serious, but with Joanne I could just enjoy her enjoying it. Joanne was all honky-tonk. My favorite serious piano player, though, was Liberace. I could have listened to him all day, every day, and been a completely happy woman.

He was incredibly handsome every single time I saw him on television, and he always talked so nice about his mama. You just don't hear that anymore, men who speak well of their parents, especially mothers. Slick's family always did about their mama, and I'm grateful for that family mercy, but the younger nieces and nephews now talk so badly of their parents. Slick's family didn't give me the same courtesy, though, I must say. They always treated me like I was trespassing on their property by marrying him. But I've tried for years to keep my mama's memory alive, to honor her by keeping her room like she left it, to share stories of things she used to say. But they don't pay mind to any of that.

It was the same with Liberace. I would talk about something I'd heard him play on television or one of his new records, which I always bought, and they would look at me like I had two heads or something. And Liberace was a Catholic's Catholic, so you'd think they would have loved him!

From time to time, I heard people poo-poo Liberace, and it always made me so mad. I'm entitled to say that he is the greatest piano player who ever lived. My forever day was years before I had to endure little Jenny making fun of Liberace and how popular he was. She started learning so much about music that somebody like Liberace didn't mean anything to her anymore. That's when I think a person just knows too much. Jenny and I were already miles apart by the time she went off to college so young and was such a success. Liberace made more money than any piano player who ever lived, so I think that should count for something. I mean, she knows so darn much about music but she doesn't make anything close to that kind of money. There were several times I almost let Slick drive me to Las Vegas to see Liberace live, but I always chickened out of going that far away from home. Of course, being the entertainer that he was, he came to Indiana several times, too, and we could have driven just two hours up to Starlight Musicals to see him in Indianapolis, but it was so hard for me to be around that many people.

I remember a night that most of the family went to see him, and they teased me for weeks about being too afraid to go. Slick was working that night, so I sat out on the front porch alone and played Liberace records while they were all seeing him up in Indy. I felt good, though, because I had my sunset birds come to the feeders and my very own Liberace concert right in my house. I pictured every moment, every outfit he must have had on. He had a twin who didn't survive being born, and I always connected with him that way, too, because my twin, Eula, never got to know the world at all. She died just a few hours after we was born. Liberace must have felt like I always did, like half a person, to lose a twin you never got to meet. When I was a little girl, people always talked about hearing Paderewski and Rachmaninoff, but Liberace could play better than them, and a lot more people knew him. I don't remember the names of all the music I heard Liberace play over the years, but I know I loved it when he played the two I could never pronounce—Chopin and Tchaikovsky. I think people forget now that when you said "Ave Maria" in the 1950s, it was Liberace who came to mind, not the Virgin Mary.

I remember first seeing him in the Soundies at the Pantheon in Vincennes, the finest movie theater around, and my jaw absolutely dropped when he played that "Tiger Rag"! I didn't know anyone could do that on a piano. And the clothes he wore! He was like some kind of mad prince you used to read about in the magazines, except he was younger than I was. He had the most beautiful clothes in the world, I think, and the people who made fun of him were just jealous. I loved how modest he always was, so different from so many of those stuffy musicians you always saw on *The Johnny Carson Show*. He pays the right respect to the President or to Queen Elizabeth, which I think is very nice. We've lost too much respect in the world. When he appeared on *The Kate Smith Show*, I thought my life was complete: my two favorite artists together. I always had to turn him off, though, before he played and sang his final song, "I'll Be Seeing You," as it was just too much for me, reminded me too much of the years Slick was away at the war and of all the boys who never came home.

CHAPTER 61

I told Jenny, "If you work hard now at learning the piano and learning all about music, you won't have to slave away like all of the rest of us have had to. Imagine being able to wake up every day and make music for a living! Wouldn't that be wonderful?" I meant it, too. All my life I wanted to play the piano and write songs, but I could never get there. I just didn't have the talent for it. I always imagined I would learn it eventually, but I never did.

Jenny told me proudly she was taking piano lessons from the nuns. Her parents were devout Catholics, or so they claimed to be. At any rate, it didn't surprise me that they wanted her to study with the nuns. They were the strictest and they did know their music, I'll give them that.

I told her, "Yes, your mama told me about that and I think it is wonderful. And I can hear you improving every day you are here. It must feel wonderful to be able to read music."

She said, "I can help you, Aunt Birdie. It isn't so very hard."

I told her I was too old now to learn anything as hard as music. I can't understand things that stand in for other things, like the way notes are written down to tell you what notes to play. I can only really bear the things that are what they are. I had to confess to her that it was beyond me, and that was embarrassing enough, but I could not stand to think about my teenage niece teaching me something I'd been trying to learn for over sixty years. I'd bought every "learn to read music" scheme there was but none of them worked. I guess in the long run it would have been easier just to learn it the long way, since none of the short ways got the job done. Jenny read music right from the start, no problem at all, at age four or five, while I struggled with it my whole life. I decided I was just going to enjoy her enjoying it, and not worry about what I knew I'd never learn. If I made a conscious decision right then and there *not* to learn it, I'd be spared the embarrassment of not knowing something in front of my niece.

The nuns shared their music teaching, but before long Jenny started working just with Sister Sheila at the Monastery of the Immaculate Conception in Ferdinand. Sister Sheila spoke with such a thick German accent that I could hardly understand a word she said the one time I met her. I'm not good with those things, but I swear I could hear Jenny starting to slightly imitate Sister Sheila's talking. I'm glad, though, that little Jenny was getting to talk about music in a way she understood, and a way that challenged her. I was sure, early on, that all those music lessons would eventually take her away. But until that day, I loved having my favorite niece around as much as I could; I only wish that time would have lasted forever.

CHAPTER 62

I noticed that Sister Sheila moved quickly with Jenny, both to get her as a student but also to move her playing along. The difference every week was an amazing thing to hear. She went from being able to play every bit of sheet music I had, and any hymn, to playing things like you heard Liberace play. It wasn't long into her studies when Jenny started talking to me about operas, so I know those ideas were put there by the nuns, too. Pretty soon Sister Sheila was meeting with great seriousness with both of Jenny's parents, who always let me in on everything. Sister Sheila was the best music teacher around here, so when they showed me the letter—"Your daughter has a greatly gifted ear for music, and I want to train her. I believe she could have a wonderful future career as musicologist and potentially, a composer"—I was thrilled. I still don't have the slightest idea what a musicologist is or does, but if it made Jenny happy, then I hoped she would look into it.

Jenny was already miles beyond any of the ladies who taught music in Ophelia, the ones who played the organ for church or who used to play the musicales at the Shawnee Opera House. There's only a few of them left, anyway, and they are all so old they don't play anymore. I'd hoped that Jenny would be satisfied enough with her talents that she would stay and teach music at the school, or at least teach piano and organ to the local girls. We just don't have the amount of music around now that we used to, and this is part of the darkness that I knew was growing in the world.

CHAPTER 63

"The Twelve Days of Christmas" was my favorite Christmas song because it was mostly about birds. I never knew my grandmama, but Mama learned the song from her, right from the old country, where there were always four *colly* birds, not *calling* birds, and we always sang it the right way in my house. I had several sets of salt and pepper shakers of the whole song, and I had a beautiful Christmas display that I found at Block's in Indianapolis that animated the whole song, with all the right numbers and everything. It was the one time of year when people thought about birds, even if they didn't really give the birds in the song a second thought. The song is about giving people living birds to keep and love, but most of the people I know thought the song was about giving birds to people so they could eat them! Can you imagine?

I did *not* like how some singers tried to fiddle with the song, like the Andrews Sisters and that hateful Bing Crosby. I just know he was not nice to birds. In the old country Mama said they used to serve a Christmas goose, but I could hardly stand that. Turkey was bad enough: every time I thought about all of the slaughtered turkeys in November my heart just about cracked in half. Over the years I got Mama and Slick to settle on chicken for Thanksgiving and Christmas because at least the chickens were being killed for eating, anyway. It was the mass slaughter of geese and turkeys that I could feel through the telephone lines. Doesn't that just sound crazy? I know it does but that is exactly how it felt to me. Every November and December in the telephone office, you could feel the pain coming through the lines. There was a lot of other December pain, of course, of lonely older folks at holiday time, of people missing their families not coming home for Christmas, but because of all of that most people didn't notice the anguish of the birds in that time of year. Most of the birds were migrating and on the move, trying to find food, hoping they had enough energy to make it to somewhere warm.

CHAPTER 64

When a person dies, you stay right where you are with them, right where you'd been all along. All these years later, I am still exactly the same with Mama even though she's been gone for so long. The birds knew this and tried to tell me long ago. I always knew it but didn't understand it completely until I got here. I'll never forget the morning Mama died. I knew something was wrong because I didn't smell any coffee, and she always started her day with making the coffee. I went to her room and there she was. Dead. Cold. She was just no longer alive. She looked like she was asleep. I said "like she was asleep" for years later whenever I would talk about it because that is what people said back then.

I always loved her name. Beulah Borders. She was named after the old hymn, and I loved to sing it. Sometimes I would just sing it by myself when I was listening to the birds.

O Beulah land, sweet Beulah land!
As on thy highest mount I stand,
I look away across the sea
Where mansions are prepared for me
And view the shining glory shore
My heaven, my home forever more.

All of Mama's fine linens were in her room, our second bedroom, and I let it sit untouched for years following her passing in 1952. She was so much a part of our lives that I still see her in everything, all these years later, however many it has been now.

I refused to alter a single thing about her bedroom. Every piece of linen, undergarment, jewelry, and all of her clothes were regularly laundered and returned to their rightful places for the next fifty years. One of Mama's dolls that she'd had for years, which always used to open its eyes when you stood her up, would never open her eyes again after Mama died. I just know that doll was paying tribute to Mama.

A lot of the family tried to get me to donate Mama's things to the less fortunate, arguing that there were many in the county who could get use out from them. That might have been true, but I wasn't going to let all them people in town wear my mama's things. They were just fine where they were and they gave me comfort being home. I kept her room and everything in it exactly as it was the morning she died, because I'd read in one of my magazines that Queen Victoria did that when her husband died. I felt I owed her that much tribute, at least.

The nieces and nephews would sleep in her room, and I loved having them, but they were never allowed to touch anything in the room. I kept a plastic mattress cover under the sheet because some of them wet the bed and I didn't want a ruined mattress. I kept Mama's bedspread, covered with pink robins, even though it did not age too well and I should have probably replaced it in the '60s, but for the kiddies it was fine.

She had a little bit of jewelry that she loved, and it is quite something to think that she had anything at all, having raised us all by herself by taking in sewing and working odd jobs like making buttons at the button factory, made from shells they pulled out of the river, until Slick and I could take her in once we got married and her back went bad. Mother-of-pearl buttons meant the world to me because I never knew exactly which ones Mama had made. I always imagined she made all of them, but over the years our clothes got fixed with newer buttons and eventually I couldn't tell them apart, and I didn't like that at all. Mama's little button box in her room was precious to me because I knew she had personally made all of them.

CHAPTER 65

They sent me in another note to say that they knew of people who forgot things for a while, but usually the memories would return. They said that some people forgot because of a kind of trauma. They said to keep the note and reread it from time to time in case it would help me. I lose the papers but I always remember what was on them. Do they think I'm having trouble remembering just because I'm staying in my forever day? That April was so beautiful that I can surely stay there if I want to.

CHAPTER 66

Spout Springs was a picnic area just a little ways down river from the Pinnacle. The largest party the area had ever seen was planned for the end of the war, when I was just eighteen, and I worked for days on two apple pies to take to the picnic. For weeks all the girls were talking about nothing but Spout Springs, for they would finally have the chance to see all of their friends who had gone off to Europe to fight. Ophelia was spared the devastation of most of the Indiana counties, if only because there were so few of us to begin with. Only one boy I knew died in the war, and he was from a distant part of the countryside, having gone to a country school, not to the five-story brick schoolhouse in Ophelia, across the river from the Pinnacle, where I'd spent so much of my girlhood days.

I'd heard of Jerry Ballard since sometime around 1918 and I was wary of him right from the start, knowing where he came from. His daddy was big money over around the big luxury hotels, and in the early '20s his Papa even bought The West Baden Springs Hotel, which was unimaginable to any of us. It was close by in miles, but it might as well have been on the moon for people living in Ophelia. There had been hotels over there for years, from even before when Mama came from the old country. After Trinity Springs went bust, French Lick and West Baden got even more popular. We'd been over there to the circus a few times. I couldn't imagine why Ballard's son was interested in me, but he asked Mama if he could take me to the big picnic at Spout Springs, and it was as much to celebrate there being no more flu cases as it was about the end of the war.

The hotel had been a hospital all through the end of the war so they weren't making any money for a while, but I'd heard tales of the Ballard boys and their spending, and I knew he'd expect some spooning from me that he was never going to get. If you jumbled together all the money in Ophelia, it still wouldn't equal what those Ballard boys had. Jerry wrote a note on hotel stationery to ask Mama's permission to take me to the party. She asked me if I wanted to go with him and I told her yes. He made me afraid but I guess not enough to say no.

If you've never seen the dome at West Baden, it is hard to imagine the greatness of it. Even as you approach the place, you can see that it is there, but nothing can prepare you for the way it draws you to the center of the building from the outside, and how it draws your gaze heavenward once you are inside it. Oh my, there is just nothing like it in the whole world that I've ever seen. They all called it the Eighth Wonder of the World and it was; even when you were standing inside it, you just couldn't believe it was real. It isn't like the dome of the U.S. Capitol, which I always wanted to see but knew I never would, because West Baden doesn't have any purpose in life other than to be beautiful. And, naturally, for people to take the waters from the springs, and they paid through the nose for it. That Sprudel Water, as they called it, smelled like rotten eggs and must have tasted worse, but I guess it made you poop, because people came from all over the world to pay for the privilege. Someone decided to create it, and aren't we always taught to be in awe of creation?

CHAPTER 67

I knew what the dome hovered over: it was one of two grand hotels that gave the perfect cover to all kinds of gambling and lechery and, I'm sure I guessed correctly, everything that comes with that. There was no way to keep that secret in our little towns, especially not when you work as a telephone operator. Did Jerry Ballard suspect I knew something from working at the telephone office? I couldn't imagine that he knew where I worked, but nothing was secret. The big-city people, especially the ones from Chicago, could sweep down into southern Indiana and get away with anything. Those awful gangsters in Chicago had to have a safe getaway, a place to plan out their heists undetected.

The only time I was ever in that hotel as a girl I walked around the first level and there was meeting room after meeting room. What did they need all that for? I know sometimes businesses went to hotels to have their meetings, but this was more than that. I found two robins trapped in the lobby that day, both of them terrified being enclosed in the huge dome, flying low to high the whole time I was there instead of staying at the tree line where they liked to be. I can still see them in my memory. I worked to get them out of there, to set them free, because I could tell from the way they were flying they weren't going to live very long in the panic of being imprisoned where they weren't supposed to be. I never liked West Baden after that, though I was in there a few more times before it all shut down after the crash, though it lasted a few years longer than it should have simply because they had a lot of Chicago mafia money behind them. Ballard even made a big public show of not selling the hotel to bootleggers and signing it over to the Jesuits. That snake-oil salesman! But I will hand it to the priests: they kept that place open for thirty years, longer than Ballard ever did.

I had the two warm pies in a cardboard box on my lap when Jerry Ballard picked me up in one of the only privately owned cars in the whole area. I couldn't begin to figure how he got so much money so young, and I wondered why he hadn't been in the war, but I couldn't bring myself to ask him. It didn't feel like he got in under the age limit.

"My father is the manager of The West Baden Springs Hotel, and he bought a dozen cars for the hotel," Jerry said. "He walked into a showroom in Chicago and wrote a check for twelve cars."

"I can't imagine," I said in honest wonder. Then, "Why do you come all the way over here when your daddy runs that huge hotel over in West Baden?"

"Daddy likes to be able to get away from work, so he built a weekend getaway house not far from here; he liked the river bluffs so we built a place nearby. It's not really that far over to the dome; it's just a lot of hills between here and there. I can take you over in this here car whenever you want."

I laughed. "Oh, I don't want to go to that place. That is for all those rich gangsters from Chicago."

He didn't smile. Then he asked, "What does your daddy do?"

"He died in an accident a few years ago. He was hit by a train just down the road there," I said, holding back tears. I always found it easier to say he was hit by a train than to explain what really happened.

"Oh, I am so sorry, Birdie. I shouldn't have asked," Jerry said sweetly.

"I like to remember him. He was the greatest man I ever knew." I could never believe people who didn't remember the dead. Even at eighteen, when I knew very few people who had passed, I remembered them every day.

We drove past dozens of brightly dressed people walking toward Spout Springs. A few of the groups yelled at the car as we passed, and every word mortified me. I hated attention, especially from men.

"Well, I still think you should come over to the hotel sometime," Jerry said.

I knew what he wanted because of something in his voice, and I couldn't bear the idea of having to drive all that way to be alone with him. Suddenly, within sight of the picnic area, I was so petrified and my head was throbbing; I felt like the day I'd been taken to the doctor in Bedford all those years before, when I was so scared. I didn't want to yell, as there were so many people around and it would be humiliating to arrive in one of so few cars only to scream and have everybody remember that for the rest of my life.

When Jerry stopped the car next to the few other cars that were there, something straight ahead caught our eyes: over a ravine a group of boys had hung a long rope and they were propelling themselves across it, like in the Tarzan stories. The ground was smothered with leaves and the trees empty, and the boys could see their way through the dense forest of naked trees. As each boy crossed the distance between two outcrops of rock, there was a lot of cheering and laughing.

"Look at that, Birdie! Look at those boys!" Jerry yelled, laughing, looking like he wanted to join them.

I'd known Spout Springs my whole life, but only as a forest of silence overlooking the silent movement of the river. Being there with so much noise and extra energy that didn't belong there filled me with dread. And they was all boys. I tipped that entire box of pies backward onto my pink dress. I tried to act like I was laughing, even though the pies were still hot and they burned.

"Birdie, are you all right?" Jerry said as he looked at the pile of beige cooked apples all over me.

"I'm fine, Jerry. I'm just so stupid for spilling these pies all over myself. I am so sorry but you are going to have to take me home. Oh my Lord!" I roared with laughter, even as I was dying inside.

"I will take you right home to change your dress," he said, and he quickly drove me back to Ophelia.

I let him drive me back, but I knew I would never return to that car, and I would never go back to Spout Springs, either, and I never did. I would only ever see Jerry again from afar, when he had other girls in his car, and many years later I would see him in the newspapers, after the hotel closed and he moved back to Chicago. Something kept him tied to southern Indiana, though, because he seemed to always be in the news.

CHAPTER 68

E ven much later, when Slick and I visited the French Lick Hotel, and passed the old dilapidated West Baden Springs, I never spilled any of my early history with the place. I was happy to walk through the sidelines full of silent knowledge. I heard tales of the old salt licks identified in the area, and there were several things in magazines about it, but they never meant much to me. I pictured great flocks of deer lapping away on the open spots of land, long in the past, and I could see how happy the birds must have been in those days. If I really thought about them, inside my silence, I could see them, each busily at their work, each worriedly cocking their heads toward the rare intruders, where eventually two grand hotels would stand, an avoidable intruder into their world. The men in those hotels ruined it all.

CHAPTER 69

I didn't open the door to salesmen, so the only people who ever called on us were family or priests, and the only people who stayed were nieces or nephews, save the dreaded times the nun came to visit. I never let anybody else in our house. And most every visit by anybody revolved around our dining room, where I kept my collection of salt and pepper shakers. By the 1970s I had stopped counting how many sets I had, but it had to be approaching a thousand, and I didn't get any more after my forever day. It kept me busy trying to keep them dusted.

I started collecting them before the war, when I saw the cutest set in a flea market up by Bedford of Little Black Sambo dressed as a maid and a chef—just adorable. We all thought little Black Sambo was cute then, and it never occurred to us that it was somehow not very nice, the way it became later. Then I started seeing different salt and pepper shakers everywhere, so my collecting took on a life of its own. People gave them to me as gifts, too, so of course I had every possible bird shaker set you could think of. But I also had over three hundred Christmas sets, as they were very popular in the '50s. I had every major President and First Lady, with lots of Kennedys, a little dog salt shaker lifting his leg on a pepper fire hydrant, a toaster with salt and pepper slices in it, mice and cheese, a hat stand with salt and pepper hats, every possible animal from every country, and I even had some dirty ones stuck away in the dining hatch so the kids couldn't see them: one lady had removable salt and pepper breasts, and I even had a priest and a little boy. Imagine if one of the nuns or priests saw that!

The shakers made me feel a little artistic, which is about the only thing I ever wanted out of life. There was no art in talking to the birds, no matter how hard I tried, and anyway it was the birds talking to me, not me to them. I also loved to make them monkey dolls out of socks. Now Jenny says they are racist! I don't think they are racist. I mean, they are just socks and nobody means anything by them. They have big lips but that is only because the socks you buy to make them have big lips. We made them out of old socks during the Depression, because the socks were cheap, not because we didn't like black people! People are so sensitive now.

CHAPTER 70

I remember one night like it was yesterday. It might have been the night of my forever day; I'm not sure. But I was showing little Jenny the slides of some of the big cities. I said, "I never understand what they do in New York or in any of them big cities. Look at Paris right here in this slide: I mean, just look at all of them people! How can anybody be around that many people? I mean, where do they buy their groceries?"

"They have grocery stores, just like we do," Jenny said.

"I know they must, but with all those people it must be so crowded all of the time."

"And they go to cafés, Aunt Birdie, and sit outside and smoke and drink and have wonderful long conversations with each other."

Now, where did she learn such a thing? I said only, "I always thought I'd like to go to Rome," knowing I'd never set foot in the place.

"I'll take you there someday." She sounded like she thought that was true.

"Oh, no—I could never go there. They don't speak English and, anyway, how would I get there?"

"We'll fly there in a jet. It is quicker than driving to Florida."

"I'm never going to drive to Florida, either," I said, meaning it. "I've seen those slides of Florida. I don't need to see alligators up close!"

"You should. My parents took me to Florida, remember? And we went to the Smokies. It was easy to get there." Jenny talked comfortably about traveling and going to strange places, almost like she preferred it to being at home.

"We drove down there to Chattanooga, where you can see seven states from Lookout Mountain," I said. "I have the slides I can show you, some of them we took ourselves."

And she said she wanted to see them, which made me very happy.

CHAPTER 71

Most of the TV shows I really liked got canceled, especially the nighttime version of *The Kate Smith Show*. I didn't think I'd ever get over the loss of that one. I planned my working hours at the telephone office in the early 1950s around getting home at 4:00 p.m. to see her daytime show. I reckon she was the greatest singer who ever lived. I remember during one of her shows the sound went out of our TV set and I just watched her hands the whole time. I could still tell what song she was singing without any sound. Jackie Gleason was on one of her shows, and he conducted a new piece that he wrote and it was absolutely amazing. How did the entire country not watch that and just fall in love with him and with Kate? I never did understand it.

Her show was only on for a few months in the early 1960s. The *TV Guide* that summer said that her ratings had been low because rock-and-roll had taken over, and there were fewer people who knew and loved Kate Smith. Whenever people on television talk about postwar this or that, or some long trends that are happening, I'm never very good at that. But I do know that when the world didn't hear Kate Smith's voice anymore, it wasn't as good a world. I wasn't ever very good at describing it, but I remember on one of her shows she sang that song Ethel Merman made famous, "They Say It's Wonderful," and it was the most beautiful thing I ever heard. When she sang I could hear every color in the rainbow, and she made certain words so beautiful. Ethel Merman sang in black and white. I always turned the television off when she was on; she was just brash and awful. It's funny: Jenny loved Kate Smith and Stevie didn't, but Stevie liked Liberace and Jenny didn't. I guess that meant something.

After the second war, I went to very few movies because there was too many to choose from and too many of them were dirty. But the biggest thing for me was that the birds were never right, so I went to films that were set indoors, and I watched those on television, anyway, so I wouldn't have to go out. I would occasionally be convinced by one of the nieces or nephews to go to a famous movie, but it always took a lot because the crowds scared me. *The African Queen* drove me insane because I just knew the bird sounds were not African. I had listened to my bird records for years, and I knew all of their sounds. I may not have had a memory for words but I sure could remember bird songs. My nephews convinced me years after my forever day to see *Raiders of the Lost Ark*, the first movie I'd been to in ages but the moment it started I knew I was hearing Australian kookaburras, even though the scene was supposed to be South America. "How am I supposed to concentrate? The birds are all wrong!" I kept saying, and pretty soon they made me leave because they said I was disturbing people.

I saw maybe one movie a year, usually whatever was being talked about the most. I also gave in and went to *Mary Poppins* when it was new because Jenny begged us to let her see it and her parents didn't seem to mind. I thought the magical parts, as the papers talked about it, were a little much for a girl as young as she was then, but her parents didn't seem to pay it much mind. I could never deny anything to the nieces and nephews, but I'm always surprised at what their parents would allow. I figured that a Disney movie would be wholesome enough, especially since movies had gotten so smutty. Jenny loved it but I couldn't figure that movie out for the life of me. I just could not enjoy it. Flying maids and chimney sweeps and rich parents? I thought London looked very pretty in the movie, but I knew I'd never see it, anyway, so it didn't make me no never mind. Jenny, though, vowed then and there not only to visit London but also to live there someday! I couldn't imagine a young girl thinking such a thing, especially not a young girl from Ophelia, but it always made me chuckle when Jenny would dream so big, which she had always done, even when she was so tiny her feet wouldn't reach the pedals. Who would ever have thought that girl would one day live in Paris, and she tells me she sometimes goes to London on the train. I don't know how that works, but it sure sounds amazing.

I loved all the songs, and I could listen to that Julie Andrews all day, but none of the birds in *Mary Poppins* was real. They had robins that sang with Mary in one of the songs but they were fake. The film even had a woman who fed birds in front of a church, St. Paul's Cathedral, but I did not like that they made that woman look crazy for wanting to take care of the poor city birds. I don't feel at all out of the ordinary for buying loaves of bread for the birds of Ophelia, and I certainly didn't ask others to pay for it like the silly old woman in the movie. The song was pretty, but it made fun of the lady for having simple words. What is wrong with simple words?

Then they had an awful scene with the penguins that made them look sweet and bumbling, when penguins in real life are terrifying. Mama took me to see the penguins at the Cincinnati Zoo before the first war, when I had begged her to take me there to see the last surviving passenger pigeon. Mama had never forgotten the sight of the great flocks of passenger pigeons that flew so thick over southern Indiana, darkening the sky even at high noon. Mama told me about Grandmama taking her to the Pinnacle to watch them for hours, an endless river of birds in the sky. The flocks were much smaller by the time she showed them to me, but I did see some and I can't imagine what they looked like when they were smaller. What I saw made you think the sky just wasn't big enough to hold them all. Mama read in the paper that all of the passenger pigeons had been killed off except for a few in the Cincinnati Zoo, so she felt she had to go pay her respects to those birds since she'd gotten such pleasure from them.

But them penguins! I remember all the people talking about how cute they were but they were not cute at all. I could divine them the minute I stepped in front of their part of the zoo, and they were mean. Maybe it was because they were cooped up so far from where they were supposed to be.

CHAPTER 72

I never forgot that trip to Cincinnati, especially the sweetness of the time on the train with Mama. There was no way to ever improve on that memory of Cincinnati so, even though we lived fairly close by, I never went back there, even when Slick wanted us to go. I just couldn't do it. My whole life I wanted to carry the memory of those gorgeous green hills and the great views of the Ohio River from some of their parks. I could have shown that to my nieces and nephews and shared it with them, told them about the passenger pigeons and the penguins, but it just made me too sad to relive the sadness of Mama's passing. Funny, over time it is the happiest memories that make you the saddest.

We are born knowing only about life, so it's no surprise that we fear dying. It is so scary to pass over because we don't know what we are passing into. I have to believe that I will be reunited with Mama and Slick, and that I'll have my forever days to relive as many times as I want. I have to believe this because it has been the only thing I've known: my forever days. Remembering them is the same is reliving them, and since I got here I wonder if we don't just reckon things the wrong way. Maybe those forever days really are forever. Maybe when we dip our minds back into them they are actually just happening at that moment. Why wouldn't my eight-year-old self, perched on the Pinnacle looking at the flocks of birds, be able to say something to me now, seventy-five or ninety years later? We are the same woman, after all. Sometimes I think I have some awfully crazy ideas.

CHAPTER 73

If I hadn't had all the bird feeders at the house, I just know I would have gone right out of myself. I don't really know how long birds live, but I know that I saw and knew several generations of birds in our yard and in the park. Oh, how I love that park, so much so that I still go there, but it hurts me that so few people use it. I knew very well who in town was having an emotional time, and they was usually the only people I saw at the park. If they'd gone there more often, they might not have gotten into such pain. It is such a pretty and peaceful place for the birds. The birds were my church. Well, first they saved my life. I feel freer to say that now. So often people would either laugh at me or just dismiss the comment, not even hear it.

Now, peregrine falcons are the most terrifying birds there are, and they have to be feared because they kill other birds and have even been known to carry off a small dog or cat. Well, I wouldn't mind if they carried off a few *more* cats. I wasn't ever very good at the names of birds, but I knew it was some kind of falcon or hawk that saved me all those years ago and it was the biggest bird I've ever seen close up. I'd never seen that exact bird before or since, anywhere around Ophelia. But I owe my life to it, and that is God's honest truth. I was saved by something that terrified me. Now, I don't mean "saved" in the way all everybody means the word nowadays. I mean it quite literally. I'll tell it for real when they make me. We are all like the Lord in that suffering is our teacher.

CHAPTER 74

For me the greatest music came from the big bands during the second war. I was only able to get through the war by sitting in our enclosed front porch listening to records. I couldn't listen to the radio in those years because the news was so terrifying and I could not hear one more word about Adolf Hitler. When Slick was away at the war, I would come home from work and listen to records for hours. And so many of those songs felt just like the birds: they would ask and answer, up and down, ebb and flow, tense and relax, all the time. Glenn Miller was my very favorite, especially that "Moonlight Serenade," which I might have listened to every night for the rest of my life. I would only listen to "Sing, Sing, Sing" when I was alone because the song felt so decadent and suggestive.

Every December 15th I would listen to Glenn Miller records all day, as that was the day he went missing in action over the English Channel. I would never get on a plane because that is how Glenn Miller and so many others died, and nothing anybody said was ever going to convince me otherwise. I loved the first recording he made of "Moonlight Serenade" because it was slower and sadder than the later ones. The clarinets, and maybe saxophones, I think that's what they were called, would answer the questions, and the trumpets, definitely the trumpets, would answer them. I would always remember that Bluebird label of that first "Serenade"; such a cute little bird. I knew I was supposed to like the Andrews Sisters, and listening to them was endurable, but I couldn't watch them in movies or on television. They was just too risqué, and that meant to me that when they got older they had to be pitied, and I don't think anyone should ever want to be pitied.

My other favorite song was quite old, and a beautiful one at that: "Toyland" by Victor Herbert. No matter how often I played and sang it as a child, my eyes filled with tears from the perfection of it: the words and the music. They were absolutely the most beautiful ever:

Childhood's joyland,
mystic and merry Toyland.
Once you pass its borders,
you can never return again.

It was an easy enough song for me to manage at the piano, and I always loved to play it. As a wedding gift, Mama gave me a music box that played it, and it was my favorite possession. I kept it in a special place on my dressing table and played it every wedding anniversary. The way it would wind down, each note getting farther and farther apart, was something I could only take once a year. My biggest regret in life is not learning how to read music or how to exercise my fingers so that I could really play. That's the only thing I ever wanted to do in my life that I didn't. I kept thinking there would be time.

CHAPTER 75

Slick came home for good on a cool autumn night in 1945 almost two months after the Japs surrendered, and I knew the night he got home that we would never spend another night apart and we never did. He called me from the train station in Vincennes before he got on the last leg of his journey home. I had never been so happy in my whole life, waiting there at the Ophelia station for him. For that one time, I was able to be at that station and not be overcome with sadness about Daddy. I'd bought a 78 of Doris Day singing "Sentimental Journey" at Palmer Electric, and I'd listened to it every day after it came out in 1944 until the end of the war. That song got me through.

On Slick's first night home, before I cooked him his favorite meal, pork chops, I rushed to put it on the record player. But even before Doris started to sing, Slick burst into tears. He tried to explain that they would play it sometimes at the camp and it always made him so homesick that he couldn't hear it without crying, but his sentences turned to tears. I'd never seen him cry before. And that night he came home from the war, he didn't just cry, he sobbed and sobbed, reaching for my arms whenever I was nearby. I quickly turned the stereo off. He was a changed man.

"Sweetheart, I'm so sorry the song made you sad."

"It isn't just the song, Birdie."

"What is it?"

"You can't imagine what has happened to the world, Birdie-wordy. So many boys who'll never be home again. And I'm home. I'm finally home. I never thought I'd see this house again."

"You are home, Slick. And you are safe. And you have a job."

"I don't know if I can work. I will do my best."

"Of course you can work, my darling. That station down at the junction is perfect for you."

During the war, I heard a lead over the phone lines about the Sunoco station down on the corner needing a manager, and I called the owner back within minutes and got that job for Slick. Yes, I heard about the job before it was posted, just like Hedy always said, but I didn't see that it mattered much if he could do the job, which he most certainly could.

But the thing I could never understand or explain was that there was a bird in one of the feeders at that time, right after the war, who would come to porch and sing the melody of "Sentimental Journey." That bird had been around while I was playing the record every day for months at a time, and when Slick said he couldn't hear it anymore, that bird took it over. It sounds ridiculous but it is God's truth. I told everybody at the time but they didn't believe me. Why should they? But it sure would have helped later if they'd believed me.

CHAPTER 76

Jenny went up to a church music workshop in Rensselaer, up at St. Joseph's College in the early 1970s when she was still a little girl, and we offered to pick her up at the end of her week there. That was the farthest north I ever went by car in Indiana. I don't rightly count the trips up to Wisconsin during the war, because that was by train and most of that trip was in Illinois, anyway. I managed to avoid Chicago on almost every one of those trips because I was so terrified of changing trains in Chicago.

I couldn't begin to imagine what anybody could study about church music for an entire week. I mean, you play some hymns that people know and that is church music, isn't it? I know it was for me. I love them old hymns. Well, we went to pick her up and she could not stop talking about her week. She was so excited. I thought for the first time that she might just want to stay in Ophelia and be a church organist, and that would make me so happy. She talked nonstop the whole way back.

"They sometimes played records for mass, which was amazing. They played a record of Wagner and people danced down the aisles," Jenny told us.

I felt so stupid. "Dancing in church?" I asked her.

"It's the newest thing. It's called liturgical dance."

The only people I knew who danced in church were Pentacostals and we all thought they was more crazy than religious. But Jenny went on and on about the dancing and how much she loved it. It was on that drive back from St. Joseph's that I first realized how serious Jenny's obsession with music was going to be. That week changed her forever.

After that, there was no stopping her being a musician for the rest of her life. She didn't have much interest in the church or church music after that week, even though that was supposedly what she went there to do, but she talked of nothing but opera after that. Old operas that somehow she learned about in a library there, or she met somebody who got her interested in them. The one thing I always liked about the Catholics was they kept their people close by for life. They were very good at roping people in and keeping them there. But they did the opposite to Jenny.

After going to St. Joseph's, Jenny told me about that Bach who wrote music, and he somehow put the number fourteen in a lot of his music. I don't understand it, but I love the way she talked about it. It was one of the times she was talking to me about it that it dawned on me: I think I had fourteen forever days in my life, and I can't get past this one, which I think is my last one. In Revelation 14:8, the angel foretells the overthrow of Babylon. I often thought of the fourteen stations of the cross, reflected on them. Mama said that praying through the fourteen stations of the cross would help me understand grace and mercy, but I never fully understood that. The stations of the cross don't show much mercy, if you ask me. Every single Catholic place we went to with Slick's family, though, had their own stations of the cross that you could walk through, not just the ones in the church, but outside exposed to the weather. The nuns could name all of them without looking.

CHAPTER 77

Stevie's crazy parents always claimed some religious problem with the kind of music he liked, calling it "Godless," as though they had any right to claim to know God in anything. Stevie was more interested in the equipment than the music, it seemed to me. Gerry never came over because she hated dogs, so Stevie had a safe haven at our place. I should have known the moment Gerry told me she hated dogs that she was a no-good woman. There isn't a person on earth I would trust if they don't like dogs. That ain't right and it ain't never going to be right.

I was the only one in the neighborhood who had an ironing machine. I bought it up in Dover Hill when the cleaner's shop up there just didn't have enough business to keep going. He told me he was going to throw that machine out! So, I offered him fifty dollars for it, and you'd think I'd have offered him the key to Fort Knox. It was a big old thing, but I cleared out room in the basement for it and I used it for everything. We always had the cleanest ironed sheets, pillowcases, and table runners. Doc Chattin's wife asked if she could pay me to do all of her ironing, so I let her, even though I wasn't a laundry woman. Most people wouldn't come down to our basement, anyway, because they said they could smell Ginger's poo and pee, but I guess over the years I got to where I just didn't notice it, because I kept that place as clean as a whistle, especially when Ginger would go down there, which was really only in the winter.

I loved the ironing, though, because I could turn the TV on upstairs, way up high, and through the coal furnace vents I could hear my programs,

Days of Our Lives and *General Hospital*. I'd been following those shows since they was on the radio. I missed a lot of them in my working years, but I had all of the soap opera magazines that kept you up on the stories in case you couldn't watch. Thank goodness for those. I did eventually sneak in a little television to the telephone office that I would cover with a bunch of doilies if Mr. McGovern ever came around to inspect, which didn't happen very often.

CHAPTER 78

People don't realize that sometimes birds sing for the same reason we do, just for fun. Those are my favorite kinds of birdsongs, because you hear them on the gentle late afternoons of spring and early summer, during the twilight. Birds sing the most in the mornings, but mornings aren't fun for birds. Mornings are when they work to be sure they have food for the day, for themselves and their families. The mornings are the noisiest from birds because they are calling out to companions about where the food is. When my bird feeders are full, as I try to make sure they always are, they sing out with every bit of might they have. If birds come around that are aggressive toward the food, then their songs completely change, to ward off the birds that might steal their food. The birds in our yard knew that the food I put out for them was theirs. I know they knew it because they had ways of telling me. If the feeders were empty, if I'd forgotten to fill them, they would wake me up, not with calls but by coming into my early-morning dreams and *telling* me. It wasn't often that I could remember these dreams, but on the days they happened it was crystal clear. Of course they would *shreep* and caw if there was anything bad going on right in the area of the yard, but they also knew much more from farther away. The birds all talk to each other, and they spread the alarms around. You won't find any creature on earth more alert to danger than a bird. They are never off watch, not even at night.

Birds mourn, too. You can hear it in their songs. They mourn each other, to be sure, but they also mourn the goings-on of the world. The birds mourned John F. Kennedy, I can tell you that. And they knew it was going to happen. I can't quite understand how they could know so much and not do anything, but that is just the way of God, isn't it? I can sit at the bird feeder in wonder for all they know, and I long ago accepted that there are things I'm just never going to understand.

Right before my forever day, I found the perfect thing, the best thing I think I ever bought: a police radio that also played eight-track tapes. It fit right on my little table in the dining room, so I could hear the police radio from all over the house. Ever since I'd retired from the phone company, I missed hearing what was going on. The police radio wasn't like hearing people's phone calls, of course, but at least I had a little bit of a clue as to what was going on. The police in Ophelia didn't know I had this radio, and I'm sure I wasn't the only one to have one. They must have realized that anyone could listen in on their conversations, but from the way they talked to each other you'd have to wonder. They would say the worst things! "We've got an old fat lady up on Sycamore who thinks there's a skunk under her house. I don't know how she could tell!" and stuff like that. But most of the time, they used that police radio to talk to their wives, who'd tell them what they wanted them to bring home for dinner.

I had that police radio on all the time, so I could monitor the goings-on in town and check it against the way the birds acted. As always, the birds are the most honest guides of all. So, keeping the police radio on in the background, my little desk radio could also play them new eight-track tapes, and I soon joined several clubs that would send me tapes every month. I loved our old records out on the new front porch, of course, but these eight-tracks were a whole new way of playing music, especially for the newer stuff that was coming out. So I made a big deal out of going to a shop on Main Street in Vincennes and buying my first eight-tracks: Liberace, Jo Ann Castle, Loretta Lynn, and of course my favorite song at that time, "Honey," by Bobby Goldsboro. Even though I already had that song as a 45, it had to be one of my first eight-tracks, so I bought it again. I'll bet I played that song five hundred times in the first week I had that thing!

The memory of Jenny that I will take to my grave and beyond is her picking out that song by ear at the piano, just like she was looking right at the music, and singing every one of those sad words like she knew what they meant! She was just aping the song, of course, at that age, but she was so cute doing it. She would sit there and play it on the piano, and she would get out my song sheets and play those—songs I'd had to work on for years she could just open up and play. How I wish I could do that. She would go right through all of them, "Mockin' Bird Hill," "Bye Bye Blackbird," "The Whippoorwill Song," and my very favorite, "When the Red, Red Robin (Comes Bob, Bob, Bobbin' Along)."

I do miss those days when Jenny was little playing that piano.

CHAPTER 79

Stevie's prized possession that spring was a set of quadrophonic head-phones laced with leather, with each ear decked out with a stylish antenna that made him look like that show I used to like, *My Favorite Martian*. Those headphones cost me a pretty penny, I can tell you that. He showed them to me at a shop on Green River Road in Evansville and I absolutely could not believe that anyone would pay that kind of money for a set of headphones, but then darned if I didn't find myself buying them. He could listen to his records for hours with those headphones, and you could see him bending himself into a pretzel playing invisible instruments. Even his real instruments, his guitars, could be plugged into those headphones, so I didn't have to hear any of that anymore, so the price of the headphones was instantly worthwhile!

I never said a word to him, or to that rattlesnake mom of his, but I was relieved he was so interested in earphones, because before them he played his music so loud you could not even hear the television, and it made Ginger upset when the whole house would rattle. I even had some of my neighbors coming over and screaming at me about loud music, can you imagine? And a couple of times he played that awful music so loud that the police came and made him turn it down. I apologized until I was hoarse to every neighbor, and I took cookies down to the station for weeks after, but I couldn't tell him to stop. He just loved it so much and he'd been denied so much by that awful woman. I felt I had time to help him make up.

That Christmas before my forever day, Stevie also decided to try out a stunt with his dad's motorcycle. He didn't, of course, try it at home because he knew they would beat him senseless, so he set it up out behind our garage before I could stop him, ramps and trampolines, and God knows what. He saw that awful Evel Knievel on television do some crazy jumping stunt and he just had to ape him. I heard him try to the first jump; and owing to the miracle that he didn't die, I was able to get out there and stop him from trying it again. He was not happy that I made him stop because he just had it in his mind that he was going to do it. When I made him realize how much his stunts were going to cost me, because gas had gone to forty cents a gallon that week, he finally gave in and agreed to stop. The birds were such a cackling mess that I knew if I didn't stop him he would have died. It's hard to get teenagers distracted from something they want to do, especially Stevie, but I managed to get him interested in one of those Dixie Riddle Cups and he finally disappeared into the garage with a set of them and played with his guitars and recording stuff.

Stevie was always listening to Aerosmith, Pink Floyd, and Led Zeppelin, and talking about them endlessly. I just could never understand wanting to listen to all that screaming and loud guitar playing. That wasn't music to me. I'd rather hear Henry Kissinger talk and that wasn't saying much: he sounded like an angry bird that ate a frog.

But I noticed some other things begin around that time, too. I don't know where he was getting it, but he was starting to drink out in the garage. He must have had some high school buddies that would go a few miles away to Illinois and buy him booze. I first found a few beer bottles and didn't think much of it. I didn't even tell Slick, but as summer approached it wasn't just beer anymore, it was vodka and Scotch and bourbon and a lot of Jack Daniel's, which Slick said was cheaper. He knew I would never be able to find the cases if he put them on the highest shelves of the balcony because I was too short, and I'll admit that it did take me a while to notice them. I thought they were just more electronics. But Stevie didn't know that when *I* said "a little bird told me," it was true. The robins led me to the shelves with the booze.

That night when I put Jenny to bed, I let Stevie go out to the garage for a while before I was going to have him sleep on the couch on the front porch, where I knew he would have to get up early because the bird feeders were so loud they would wake him up at dawn. Slick and I settled in to watch *Love, American Style*, which Slick always liked even though I found it awfully dirty. That night it was Bill Bixby, who I just loved in everything, and Connie Stevens fighting about something. She was a little too racy for me, but I guess it put me to sleep.

I must have drifted off, because when Gerry phoned near midnight, my toes nearly shot through the front of my fluffy house shoes. I rushed into the dining room where the phone desk was, the one I brought home when I retired from the telephone office.

"You tell that boy to get his ass home now!" Gerry screamed. "What are you doing, keeping him over there at this hour?"

"He told me you said it was okay for him to stay over," I told her.

"I said no such of a thing," she screamed back. "Go out to that garage, Birdie, or I'll come over there and get him myself. God knows what that boy is up to."

"Calm down, now. Hang on"—and I put the phone down to rush out to the garage. Slick yelled something about who was on the phone, but I didn't stop to answer him. I opened the little side garage door but Stevie didn't stir. He was seated with his back to me at his new equipment near the back of the garage under a single bright light. He had on his headphones, the expensive ones I'd bought him. I couldn't believe he'd be able to fall asleep with that racket he listened to, which I could hear even when I opened the small door to the garage, but by God that boy was asleep.

"Stevie, your mom is calling. You should get on home."

He didn't hear me. I said it all again, louder. I had Ginger bark, but he didn't hear any of it. Finally I couldn't hear anything coming from the headphones so I figured whatever he'd been listening to had run out. I didn't understand how all his equipment worked or what it was. He had a cup sitting between his legs. I smelled liquor. He was snoring. I knew I had to wake him, as Gerry was furious on the other end of the phone line. But I got scared, because Stevie was big and strong by that time, not at all like the sweet little boy he used to be. All my memories fled back to that late afternoon at the Pinnacle, so many years before. I hadn't thought about it in years and years. I heard the birds stirring all around. I lightly touched his shoulder to wake him.

Stevie yelled himself awake as he threw the contents of the cup all over the recording equipment. The headphones came off when he jumped up, and like a reflex he pushed me out of the way, too drunk to realize what he was doing. I fell to the floor and Ginger started barking and lunging at Stevie.

"Fuck!" he screamed as his equipment started to sputter and hiss with little puffs of smoke.

I remember saying quietly, "Don't hurt me."

"Oh—Aunt Birdie—I'm so sorry. I would never hurt you. You scared me. I'm so sorry. Oh Birdie!" He was crying drunk.

"Your mom is on the phone wanting you home. I thought you was already gone. I'm sorry I scared you but I guess you fell asleep."

"I did. Are you hurt? I'm so sorry, Birdie!"

"I'm not hurt. I'm going to go back and tell your mom that you are coming home. You'd better get on in a hurry now," I said, picking myself up.

"Yes, I'll go home. Oh Birdie, I'm so sorry."

"I'll clean all this up later. You go on."

I knew he'd had too much to drink to drive, but he only had to cross the highway safely and he'd be home in five minutes, probably before I'd finished talking to his mother.

CHAPTER 80

One of the things I've noticed since I got here is that when I get nervous, I make sounds with my mouth like I was chewing gum. It's just a jittery habit that Slick blocked out completely over the years, but the sound drove Gerry nearly insane, and I think the phone probably amplified it. As I picked up the phone to tell Gerry her son was on his way home, I didn't even have a chance to speak before she screamed, "Will you stop that goddamn chewing like a cow with his cud? It drives me out of my goddamn mind!"

"Stevie is on his way home. He fell asleep in the garage listening to his music. He was going to stay here but I've sent him home."

"You're such a liar. You should have woke him two hours ago. Jesus fucking Christ!"

"I've told you not to curse in front of me. Slick and I were watching television and I got absorbed in some program, probably drifted off to sleep myself. You know how Stevie gets listening to his music and playing with his amps and things."

"I'll curse whenever the fuck I want to, Birdie. You are trying to spoil and steal that boy. Well, I'm going to ground him after I have his dad take the belt to him and tan his hide but good."

"Don't you dare hit that boy, Gerry. He's big enough now that he's liable to hit you right back." I tried to laugh, but the chewing started again.

"Stop that goddamn chewing!" Gerry roared at me.

"If you'd be a proper mother to that boy maybe he wouldn't be drinking."

"You bitch," Gerry said, and she hung up before I could admonish her again. Curse words made my chest tight, especially the really bad ones, like "goddamn" and "fuck." When Gerry let loose with a string of them, I couldn't find my breath. I hung up the phone, and it felt like there was no air in the room. I gasped and felt faint as I sped to the kitchen. I got Ginger a chocolate bar from the cabinet, hoping it might distract me from the feel of my heartbeat in the back of my throat. I tried to call for Slick, but I couldn't get enough breath under me to make any noise.

After a few minutes of drinking water, I felt I was returning to my body. I knew the birdbaths and the bird feeders all needed tending, and I knew I needed to return to the garage to clean up and try to turn everything off so there wouldn't be a fire. Ginger devoured the chocolate bar as she always did, and I took her back outside, this time with a flashlight, to do a quick run through the yard. I hosed out the two birdbaths as Ginger roamed, and I noticed something strange had taken place around the bird feeders. I first thought there might have been a fox around that scared the birds, but I hadn't seen a fox in town in years, and I knew the birds would have warned me if they'd seen something so violent as a fox. It was too big a mess to clean up when I just had a flashlight, so I decided to come back in the daylight to deal with it. I gave up on the front bird feeders as they were a mess, too.

I let Ginger roam around while I went back to the garage. I was suddenly furious with myself for not telling Stevie off but good for being drunk. Now the whole place smelled of whiskey. I started turning off all the buttons I could see. There were lights on nearly every machine in the garage. The one thing I couldn't figure out how to turn off was the board with the levers that he'd spilled his booze all over, so I left it on. It had stopped sputtering smoke and just smelled of warm Jack Daniel's, which made me want to retch.

I turned out the garage light and noticed something on the ground that I hoped wasn't a snake. It seemed small for that, but you never know in Indiana. I didn't see so good at night. I picked it up and it was a plastic cord that connected to some big thing. He'd dropped those expensive headphones in a little speck of mud and they were filthy. I picked them up to take them in for a good cleaning.

I called for Ginger, since it was nearing midnight and I was almost never outside at that hour. As I climbed the back porch steps, I heard birds in the huge walnut tree and wondered what they were stirring about. From behind me came a voice that scared me out of my wits.

"What the hell do you think you're doing with those?"

It was Stevie. Drunk. He looked like he'd been beaten up. He made me scared.

"Honey, why are you bleeding?" I asked him.

"Because Dad beat the holy shit out of me for drinking and I left." Stevie laughed.

"Oh, I hate that," I said, hoping he wouldn't come in. "Are you going to stay here?"

"I can't very well go home now, since you decided to spill the beans on me to Mom and Dad," Stevie said, angry.

"I didn't. Your mom called here, and I was asleep. I forgot you was out here. I'm just going to clean up your headphones. You dropped them in the mud," I said, nervous.

"I didn't drop them anywhere, you old tattle-telling bitch."

I was so scared then. "Stevie, you mustn't say those things. You've had too much to drink."

"I'm going to drink a lot more. Let me in the garage. I'll stay out here tonight."

I half wanted to let him stay in the garage just to have him out of the house.

"There's no place for you to sleep out here and it is getting cold. You should come in and sleep on the front porch couch. You'll sleep like a little baby out there," I said, hopeful.

"I know you don't want to get hit again, old woman. Let me in that garage," Stevie said, barely able to stand up.

"I've thrown out your booze so there's nothing left in there."

He lunged at me and tripped over the bottom step, hitting his head. He started laughing and I could have killed him for that. "You get yourself cleaned up and get to bed. This is enough nonsense from you tonight."

I was proud of how forceful I was with him, considering I was scared. He went in the house and collapsed on the front couch. I knew he would get blood on everything but I was glad he was down for the night and hadn't hurt himself more.

"You've got a fag for a husband and everybody but you knows it."

"What the hell are you talking about? Stop that right now. You are just talking drunk."

"Ask him what he really gets up to with the priests around here. You think you know everything, think you've heard everything from the phone office…you think the birds help you. It's all bullshit, you stupid old bitch."

"Stop it right now. Stop!"

"At least he's keeping the priests off the little boys," Stevie sneered, then laughed, "until we got old enough to fight them off ourselves!"

I couldn't believe he laughed. His words hurt me so much, even though I knew it was just the liquor talking.

I put the headphones on the kitchen counter to clean them and out on the front porch I covered Stevie up, hoping he would just sleep it off.

CHAPTER 81

I still can't believe it happened, and it plays over and over in my head to this day. I guess it always will. Where was Ginger? Oh God, no. I pleaded into darkness: not on this night, please, or any night. I never wanted Ginger to meet an end like that. It was so fast. For an instant I saw Ginger in the headlights of the car. The car tried its best to slow. Ginger looked trustingly into the headlights, trying to see what was happening to her. I saw those headlights as if they were approaching me instead of Ginger. I wish they had been. I felt the car roll over me as surely I saw it run over Ginger, and the car lost its front right hubcap as it fought against her body. Ginger didn't cry out. I screamed bloody murder. The car stopped, its driver unsure what he'd hit. I recognized the man but couldn't remember his name. He lived up the road a piece. He turned his car around so that he could see what happened, hoping against hope that she might still be alive and just have a broken leg or something. But by the time I made it to the road, I could see she was gone. I thought of Daddy all those years ago, being hit by something that fell off a train. I took Ginger into my arms, so shocked at having to say good-bye so soon, when I'd only expected to have a short walk and go to bed. I thought of Slick, who'd probably been half asleep for more than an hour and he knew nothing about this. I heard some of the birds in the big walnut tree stirring.

"My God, Birdie, I've killed your dog," said the driver. "I'm so sorry. I didn't see her."

"I don't know you. You couldn't help it. It was just one of those things that happens." I picked Ginger up. There was blood everywhere. She was heavy.

"I'm just going to bury her in the yard," I said, surprising myself.

"Now? Let me help you." He was full of grief.

"Of course now. It has to be now. What would she smell like by morning? Has to be now," I said. It feels now like I had a lot of presence of mind.

"Would you let me help you?"

"No, no. You go on. I need to put her to rest myself."

"Birdie, I feel just awful."

"I don't know you. I am going to take Ginger now."

"I'm so, so sorry, Birdie."

"I know. Good night."

I took Ginger's bloodied body far back into our backyard, near a little group of trees where she used to run to find all of her favorite birds. I was thankful that I just had on an old nightdress, because it was covered in a lot of blood. I set Ginger down on the ground and went to the garage to get a flashlight and a shovel. So much of Stevie's speakers and sound equipment looked like it was still on, I thought, but there was no time to worry about that.

I propped the flashlight nearby and began to dig. I was quickly covered in perspiration that mixed with the blood all over me. For what seemed like an hour I slowly made a dent in the earth a few feet deep. Just before I had to place her into the earth, I began to sob, quietly at first but then with great howls into the night. I took Ginger into my arms one last time, so unexpectedly on what should have been a normal evening. I took off my nightdress, which was falling apart anyway, wrapped Ginger in it as tenderly as I could, and placed her in her grave. It was over. I slowly replaced each disrupted piece of dirt back to where it belonged. I knew I would visit this place every day for the rest of my life to remember my wonderful Ginger.

CHAPTER 82

When the last morsel of earth had been replaced, I realized I'd never been outside with no clothes on. There were no neighbors close enough to see me, but what if there was some lurking prowler? Not likely, but what if that man who hit Ginger decided to come back and help me out of guilt? The thought made me hurry back to the garage to replace the shovel and flashlight, so I could get into the house and clean myself up. With no housedress on now, I wiped the sweat from my forehead and face with my hands, and I tasted something I'd never tasted before. Blood. Ginger's blood. It tasted of metal and fire, things that were of the earth. I thought I was probably also tasting some of the dirt she had disturbed. I knew I'd read somewhere some people saying amazing things about the taste of blood but was distracted by a sound coming from the garage, from Stevie's equipment, even though I thought I'd turned it all off. There was a screen with lines all over it, horizontal lines, and it was making sounds that sounded almost like words, but not quite. I thought I should turn some of these speakers and things off, but I didn't know how and didn't want to make Stevie angry. I was scared of him when he angry.

I went to the garden hose near the entrance to the back porch and tried to remove the biggest chunks of grime from my feet before I went into the house to really clean up. How could I explain to Slick and Stevie and Jenny what had gone on while they slept?

As I showered I noticed I could still taste Ginger's blood and it was sweetening somehow as the minutes passed. I watched the blood and dirt wander in little streams in the bathtub searching for a drain. I vowed during that shower that I would never have another dog. I couldn't take that kind of heartbreak again. More than just Ginger had died in that moment; some part of me, the deepest part, not just emotions and thoughts, had also begun to decay, but some other things felt stronger. Oh, how I wished I had the words to explain what it felt like!

Some people have the most wonderful words. My eyes, though, something was off about my eyes. Things were floating in front of me but they weren't like the normal little pieces of grit I saw on sunny days. These were faint wavy lines across my eye that went in all direction. For years, when I came inside from sunlight I could see my heartbeat in my eye, little pulsing veins, but those definitely looked like something from inside me. This was different. I'd never seen anything like it. I hoped it wouldn't mean a trip to the doctor. I couldn't stand doctors. I was sure it would be gone by the next morning, as my ailments always seemed to be.

Slick was still in his recliner as Johnny Carson was interviewing somebody holding an eagle, or was it a falcon? I didn't pay much attention. I woke Slick enough to walk him to the bedroom and get him tucked into our bed that only fit in the tiny room on an angle, which gave me some storage space in the corner behind it for Christmas decorations. We had so little room in that house, especially now when I think about it from here where I have all the room you could ever dream of. I went back to the kitchen where Ginger would normally be waiting like an angel for another chocolate bar. I took all them chocolate bars out of the cabinet and threw them away, sobbing. I grabbed a handful of Oreo cookies from the yellow cookie jar, and dunked each one in a glass of milk. I ate the whole jar. I then cleaned the last of the day's dishes.

I went in to check on Jenny, glad she had no idea of anything that had gone on. I realized I hadn't really been in Mama's bedroom that day, or probably for a few days, so I enjoyed the few minutes of quiet. I opened each drawer, dusted each photo, and remembered so many times with Mama. It was the afternoon picnics I always remembered first: the times with the family outside on beautiful late-spring evenings, or Mama laughing at the picnic table at Spout Springs, or that time at the overlook before they put the highway in and it was still quiet. In the stillness of that room, at that hour, I could still feel Mama arranging the bows on my dress, or tightening ribbons in my hair. I walked the doll out from the wall and started to tidy her, as the poor little thing had gone several weeks without any care. I sat on the little chair and dusted the doll's eyes, ears, and mouth, fluffed her pink dress, and brushed her hair with a special brush I kept on the bedside table.

I put the doll to bed on the little doll bed next to Jenny and began my nightly ritual on the living room couch. I hadn't slept in the same bed with Slick for years because there just wasn't enough room in the double bed for the two of us. We'd both gotten so big. And for several years I'd had trouble breathing when I was lying flat so I had a series of pillows I could keep at an angle on the couch that wouldn't put me flat. It was a ninety-degree deal and it gave me a few hours of sleep every night.

I slept for years on the couch, which everybody in the family said was not doing anything good for my back and was probably ruining the couch, too, but I had it all re-covered several times and it looked just as good as new. Jenny's parents in particular would not shut up to me about sleeping on a couch without proper back support, and how much better I would feel if I would only sleep in Mama's bed if I wasn't going to sleep with Slick. I told them I liked having the nieces and nephews over too much to take up that bed myself. What they were really trying to tell me, without saying it, was that they disapproved of me not sleeping with my husband, as though they could possibly understand any of the reasons for that.

CHAPTER 83

What I really meant was this: never once in the more than sixty years I lived in that house, including the fifty that followed Mama's death, did I *ever* spend a night in that bedroom. My nights were always the same. After Slick took himself to bed, I would make my bed on the couch, turn out all of the lights in the house, and watch the last of the day's television, which always ended with the national anthem followed by static, which I would leave on because it kept Ginger from hearing any noises outside at which she might bark. Ginger always slept in the space between the coffee table and couch. Many times I would put my hand down to pet her and she would slightly move herself.

That night, my first without Ginger, I had terrible trouble falling asleep. I was starting to be sore from having been thrown to the ground but I knew I couldn't very well tell Slick about that, and I sure wouldn't ever say anything to Stevie about it. I was anxious about whatever had caused the disturbance around the bird feeders, and even through the static of the television I could hear a birdsong somewhere that wasn't normal for that time of year. The notes were spaced real wide instead of close together like normal. I wished I knew exactly what the bird meant, but I could tell it was a warning call of some kind. I hoped the morning would bring an answer. The cuckoo clock struck 2:00 a.m. and startled me, but I was asleep before the 3:00 a.m. birdcall.

I slept a type of sleep that night that I knew well: grief sleep. In grief sleep you barely drift off, and when you do, you relive things over and over and over and over, and you think about things that happened long ago that you thought you'd forgotten. That night I dreamed of Frances Farmer even as I woke every half hour or so, and I could not figure out why I would dream of her that night. I hadn't thought of Frances Farmer in years, yet her movies were favorites from years ago. And I'd loved the local program she had in Indianapolis. Was *farmer* the word I'd heard at the Pinnacle that time? What was that word? It was something similar. Strange.

CHAPTER 84

Near dawn I realized that names really do carry magical powers. Frances Farmer was nearly the name of the woman who gave her house to Ophelia to be the first public library, Frances Folkes, around the time of the first war. Frances had no heirs and didn't go to a church. Rumor was she was a witch, but only because she went to college and didn't believe in God like everybody else, just the same as Frances Farmer. I was scandalized by some of things Frances said and did, but I admired how she spoke her mind no matter what it might cost her. If Frances Farmer had been able to talk to birds, she wouldn't have been afraid to tell everyone like I have been. In those days, you knew the rumors and the truth at the same time, and you could always tell the difference. I remember visiting Fannie as a child, but somehow her name had disappeared from my memory. But Frannie or Fannie, whatever the name was, gave her house to be a library for Ophelia, and I always loved that a person would be so generous as to do such a thing. Before I went to work at the telephone office, I'd so wanted to be the librarian in that house. It would have been the perfect job for me, as I could have walked to work, as it was only a few steps away. I could take care of all of those precious books and help people find their way to what they wanted to read. What a beautiful thing to do, to help people know things, but not too many things.

I applied for the job at the city hall. I remember how terrifying it was to fill out that application and walk up those stairs to find the office where I had turn it in. I knew they would likely want a woman as a librarian, but

I was worried because the application asked for educational credentials, and I only had my high school diploma. I'd been a good student, but in those years of the first war there was almost no way for a woman to go to college. I can't think of more than two in the town who did, and they were both from rich houses. Everybody who worked for the city would have been through the same thing as me. Still, everything made me nervous in those days. The city hall felt suddenly felt so official and serious.

"We do need someone with a college education for this job, Birdie. I'm so sorry," the fellow told me over the phone, and that was it. Why did this memory come back to me so strong while washing off my dead dog decades later? I can't figure out how these things happen to me, or how my memories work. Isn't that something that being here is supposed to help me with? When is that going to begin?

If I'd had that job, it would have changed the way my life went. Maybe, in the long hours sitting at the desk of the library, I might have had the chance to learn more about all the birds. Sometimes the birds get so loud in my head that I can't hear anything else, and I know they are trying to tell me something. Maybe if I'd had that job I would have been able to figure it out. And I wouldn't have had to work at the telephone office and know so much about everyone. I want to be able to give all of those memories back! I don't want to know so much.

CHAPTER 85

When I woke up all the way and really opened my eyes, I knew I was different. Something was new. My eyes were seeing things they didn't normally see, but it was my ears I really noticed. I was hearing birdsong that I'd never heard before, as though they were inside the house.

I heard Slick wake early, sometime between 4:00 and 5:00 I guessed, to get the station open by 6:00. He always left so early. I knew Stevie would be in big trouble at home for drinking, and since I also knew Gerry would be around at some point to yell at me again, I threw my clothes on and got back to the garage to get rid of anything that might get Stevie in even more hot water. The whole place smelled of liquor and I had to get rid of that smell. The big amplification board with the levers was still on from the night before, and it hummed quietly, a noise I hadn't noticed the night before. There was a large cardboard box on the shelf that looked suspicious so I got the ladder. It had been years since I'd been on a ladder. I peered over into the box, unable to move it even slightly; it was about full of liquor bottles, that little pissant. I decided to remove one bottle at a time since I couldn't move the whole thing.

But even one bottle of Scotch was heavy for me, and I could tell by the way my heart was racing that I couldn't possibly go up and down the ladder a dozen more times. I managed to retrieve two of the bottles, but as I went down the ladder with a third, I slipped slightly and fell onto all the levers, and a reel of tape on another board began to spin. It was a recording Stevie had made of the backyard birds. I loved birdsong so

I enjoyed it for a few minutes, and then the sounds began to change, though the tape seemed to be moving at the same speed. The liquor I had spilled had done something to the sound. Slowed down, the birds sounded like dinosaurs in drive-in movies, and their songs were so much more complicated than what we normally hear, much more so than the few intervals I tried to learn on the piano. Their songs were filled with notes between notes, sounds that humans usually can't hear, and I felt frustrated not to know more about music so I could really understand what they were trying to communicate. I didn't know how or why, but I sure knew that their songs were beautiful. Slowed down like this, though, it felt like they were keeping the greatest secret there was. These sounds are all around us every day but we can't hear them.

I had to really think through what had happened to me. Stevie had hit me. Ginger had been hit by a car. I buried her. I tasted her blood. Blood. Was it dog's blood that made me able to see what I was seeing and hear the birds? When I put my mind to it, I saw the same things the birds were seeing. And inside their songs I could hear music that no person had ever heard before. I was so excited but it was also petrifying. I was being entrusted with a message from the birds and I didn't know who to give it to or what to do with it. I couldn't very well go to the police. They would just lock me up for being crazy. Anybody in the family would just tease me about it and use it against me later. Jenny. I would tell Jenny. She always had such clear ways of thinking about things, and she would believe me. The next time she called, I would tell her. I had no idea how to call her in Paris.

I noticed a small radio on a nearby table was also making noise, maybe it had been all along, I wasn't sure. It was no bigger than my purse, and it wasn't plugged in. I'd heard about battery-powered radios but I'd never actually seen or heard one, so I decided to try out the headphones I had just cleaned. The sound was amazing. I'd never heard anything through headphones before. I turned the dials of the radio and heard sounds I'd never been able to notice in the car radio or from the large radio I kept in the kitchen. And this radio was so small that I had no trouble carrying it with me. I decided to keep it on while I went to investigate the bird feeders.

I'd never felt anything like the sensation of them headphones. I found myself walking quieter so as not to miss anything on that radio. I found the classical station out of Evansville, and it was as clear as if they were standing right there beside me—much clearer than you ever heard on the radio in the house. I guess I startled some of the birds as I came around the corner of the house, because as soon as I appeared, they all scattered in a fright. Several of them flew right by my head, so close I could feel the wind from their wings, a sensation I always loved but which you can almost never feel. As they passed, one of them nicked one of the antennas on the headphones, and I heard a very distinctive word, clear as a bell: *blaffer*. What did it mean? Did the birds speak in a kind of code?

That was the word from all those years ago at the Pinnacle. I'd heard it before and not been able to remember it.

But I heard the birds say a lot more that morning. They knew everything. Absolutely everything. I never wanted to take them headphones off. But the thing I've never been able to figure out, is that when I did take them off, I could still hear everything I'd heard when I had them on. My whole way of seeing and hearing had changed. I did not know what to do.

CHAPTER 86

Slick and Jenny still knew nothing about what had gone on the night before with Stevie or Ginger. Jenny would be getting up expecting to give Ginger her first chocolate bar of the day. Slick was already gone to the station. I got up all my courage and went to Mama's room to wake Jenny.

I'd heard it said that when you sneeze your heart skips a beat. It also skips a beat when your niece is not asleep where you tucked her in. I couldn't believe it but Jenny was not in her bed. Mama's room was empty.

I yelled her name and went through every inch of the house. I saw her at the Pinnacle but it was the same way a bird would see her. It wasn't me. Could that be right? I called Slick at the station and tried to explain through my crying what was going on. I was so scared I could barely breathe. How was I going to tell Slick's brother and sister-in-law that their daughter was missing? I was sure I would die right there just thinking about it. I went back to Mama's bedroom to see if there were any clues I could find. Slick called back telling me to call the police. I said I couldn't do that yet. Didn't want to arouse any suspicion if we didn't need to. I knew I had to call Slick's brother, so I sat down at the phone desk and tried him. He picked up right away.

"I can't find Jenny," I blurted.

"Oh, she came home early this morning and she's gone back to sleep. She just walked right in while we were having breakfast."

"How did she get there?"

"I'm sure she just walked. She's fine, Birdie, sorry she scared you."

I laughed. "Scared me half to death to walk in there and have the bed be empty!"

"I don't think it is a good idea to have Stevie stay over there when there are girls in the house," he said.

"Stevie was so drunk he didn't move off that porch."

"That isn't what Jenny told us. She's fine, but I think she should only stay over if it's just her."

"Yes, of course. You are right."

"Thanks again and we will talk at you soon!" He hung up.

I was so relieved little Jenny was okay, but something didn't feel right. I couldn't breathe. The birds were stirring. I went to front porch and Stevie was gone. I knew he wasn't in the garage. I called Gerry.

"Gerry, I have to tell you something." My voice was strong.

"What is it now, you old fool? That boy just got back home." Gerry laughed. "His Dad tore a strip through him with a belt last night, so I'm glad he's off to work. I don't want them to get into it again."

"This is serious. Stevie is too young to be drinking and you have to do something. I think he tried to do something bad to Jenny." The words nearly brought tears to my eyes.

"Bullshit, Birdie. That boy is a boy and I don't care if he takes a swig every once in a while. But that ugly little fat girl is in no danger, I can tell you that right now!" Gerry laughed again.

"Gerry, that is just a horrible thing to say about any little girl! You are fat yourself!" I couldn't believe my gumption.

"You calling me fat, you old beached whale? You sit up there and cook your pork chops for that fat dog, eating six of them yourself. I know what goes on in your kitchen."

Oh, I hated it when she sounded so sure of herself!

"A car hit Ginger last night, thanks to you."

"What did that have to do with me?"

"If I hadn't been so worried about Stevie, I'd have taken Ginger out much earlier and she wouldn't have been hit by a car. You have done some awful things in your life, Gerry, and said some awful things, but you have never been this cruel before. You horrible, hateful, bitch!"

The words fell out of me quietly, and I heard them as though I didn't say them.

"You know what? You think you know how to raise my son? Why don't you raise him? He can come and live with you. I don't give two shits either way. Is that so hard to believe?"

"No, I can believe it. That's what kind of a mother you are. Never have been worth a hill of beans."

"Calling me, trying to say that boy thinks your fat dyke of a niece is worth fighting over. Jesus H. Christ."

Oh, I hated that Gerry.

"Don't you talk like that in front of me. You should be doing right by your son." My voice was getting louder.

"I've done everything I intend to do for that boy. He's a deadbeat. He's all yours if you want him. If you don't, I couldn't possibly care less."

CHAPTER 87

The minute Slick came in the door from work that night, I knew something was wrong. He could barely make it up the few steps to the back door, he was having such trouble breathing. It had been a roaster all day, hot as Hades, and as much as I wanted him to just have a little heatstroke, I knew this was worse. I called Doc Chattin, who was there within five minutes. Right away he said he was calling an ambulance to take Slick to the hospital, about twenty minutes away. "There's no time to waste, Birdie. He is having a stroke."

I heard those words as if I was drunk. They didn't seem real to me. I remember saying, "I don't want them doctors hurting him," and begging Doc to let me keep him home just a little longer.

"He's also having a cardiac event of some kind, Birdie. He needs to be in a hospital," Doc said again.

"Heart?" I nearly exploded at saying the word.

"It's impossible to know for sure unless he is in a hospital. He could be in danger of a stroke. His blood pressure is very high and we need to discover what's causing that."

"It can't be his heart. Oh my God!" I began to cry.

"Birdie, let me call an ambulance."

"No! No! No! If you take him away, he will never come back!" I knew he wanted to stay with me, and if he was meant to die in 1973, he would want to die at home.

"Birdie, if he doesn't get to a hospital he may die here in his chair."

Slick didn't say a thing. He just sat in his chair and waited for me and Doc to decide something about him. I knew he wanted to stay home. Doc went home saying to call him if anything changed. I put Slick to bed and he went right to sleep. I didn't sleep a bit that night. I was so worried Slick might die, but I was too scared to take him to the hospital. He did seem to sleep and get some rest. His breathing was normal from what I could tell. I could hear things in him that I'd never heard before. For a while I thought I could actually hear his heart beating.

CHAPTER 88

The next morning I thought Slick got to feeling better, but I was against him going to the station. He would hear none of that. He insisted on going to work as usual. That night he wanted to drive over to Washington to play putt-putt golf, one of our very favorite things to do. We must have played that golf course a thousand times, and some of our happiest memories are still there. There is just nothing more fun than a good game of putt-putt.

As we parked and paid for our games, I convinced myself that Slick had turned a corner and was getting better. Slick wanted to go play putt-putt so we did, against my better judgment. As we almost always did, we stayed after our game and talked to the owner, Roy—I never knew his last name after all those years—for an hour or more. That man could talk about anything. He turned the lights off on the course so the mosquitoes could find meals elsewhere.

After a while Slick looked tired and was sweating as though we'd just climbed a flight of stairs. He started to slur words. Roy got him some water and we sat him down on a lawn chair for a spell. "I just got overheated; the air is so heavy," he said, sounding drunk. Roy tried to convince me to take him to the hospital that was just a few minutes away, and unlike the night before I was ready to but this time Slick wouldn't go. I tried to get him to do what I said but he insisted I drive us the few miles home to Ophelia, and I tried to keep him talking and keep an eye on his health the whole time, while trying to drive us home in the dark.

I put him to bed and he quickly went to sleep. For the life of me I couldn't settle down that night. I was so worried about him. I should have made him go that hospital. I tried to read and couldn't concentrate. I flicked through a dozen magazines and finally turned out the light. As I drifted to sleep, I heard the birds in the front trees stirring. The television test pattern was painting the walls of the living room where I lying on the couch. I saw, in and out of my grief sleep, little lights darting first in straight lines then branching out into what looked like X-rays of trees. The points of light were moving fast, like a lightning storm, but there was no noise. Little dams that had been holding the light silently burst, sending everything alight. Even in sleep I wondered where this was happening? Was it outside? Was it one of the birds? Was it what the birds saw when they looked at the world?

My dream quickly became just a longing to know what it meant. I was in a hallway that was so long I couldn't see the end of it. The birds woke me just as I heard Slick gasping for breath in the bedroom. I ran. It was 3:00 a.m. He couldn't say his own name. He couldn't walk. I remember trying to put his jaw back where it was supposed to go, but it stayed off to the side, lifeless. I tried to get him to the car, but he couldn't move and I couldn't begin to carry him. I was out of options, so I phoned the police, knowing from my years at the telephone office that they would come right over and call an ambulance from their car. Sure enough, within a minute of my call I could see the red lights of their car. Terror came over me, wondering if Slick might be dying right then and there, but also the embarrassment of those lights, knowing that all our neighbors would see Slick being taken out of our house on a stretcher.

They arrived and carried my husband away. He would return, but I'd never see all of him again. I still can't believe they wouldn't let me ride with them, but the man had one of those voices that made you listen. I knew those voices.

CHAPTER 89

Jenny came to visit often, at least once a month during her college years. She sure didn't seem like a little girl anymore when it didn't take her long to get down to business, talking about Slick's health. I told her straightaway, "Don't ever talk to me about heart disease or strokes or anything else, you hear me?"

"Birdie, you have to face some of the truths about Slick's health, and you are ignoring your own. You don't have to feel bad. There are ways to help you both."

"No! You don't understand! It's the ideas that put the disease there. If you never know about it, you won't ever get it. Everybody just needs to stop talking about it all the time."

CHAPTER 90

I couldn't reckon what brought this to mind in that minute, but the memory was so strong I could smell the grass in it. I was playing in the yard and Mama was inside washing up breakfast. Daddy had gone. It was hot out. The German reverend across the street was mowing his grass and struggling with it. The clippers were jammed or something. He stopped and wiped his forehead. I was playing with some dolls, I think, but I know I was on the grass. Trost was his name; Reverend Trost. I always remembered him because he was a kindly man who talked with an accent and his name sounded like toast so it was easy to recall. I remember the mower not moving anymore. The reverend was on the ground next to it, and everything was silent. Something was wrong but I couldn't tell what it was.

I ran inside to Mama and then those cars came, just like for Slick, with men who spoke sternly; only my memory of it is silent. The stretchers and all the people who come to help when somebody's sick…I thought of all of that. The reverend never came back, and I remember all the grown-ups talking about attacks, his heart had been attacked, and I pictured scary little men surrounding him, like gnomes in those stories, too tiny to be seen, and they all attacked him while he mowed his lawn.

Repetition is what kills people. It isn't the one cigarette you have. It is the ten thousand cigarettes you smoke in ten years that makes your body protect itself. The same is true of our inner quilt, as Mama used to call it. If we hold something in too long, it comes out as disease. If we've wronged someone but never owned up to it, we will pay for that somehow. The same goes for wrongs that were done to us without our consent. We have to own up for them and say they happened. Say it out loud, or husbands will have strokes. Something terrible had happened to Slick. Right then and there, the thing to do was to keep him alive so he could get better enough to tell me what was wrong.

The birds know about repetition. And birds are patient. They know things collectively in ways we can't imagine. They drift beautifully in the sky most of the time, often for centuries, but when they are forced they can be the most destructive creatures imaginable. I remembered going to the Pinnacle to see the great flocks that would fly directly toward us, some stopping in the trees, but most of them making big sculptures over the sky. I could watch them forever. They were the only thing I could think about as I drove to the hospital.

CHAPTER 91

Checking Slick in at the emergency room, I had to answer questions that made me very uncomfortable. When I worked at the telephone office, I heard people ask questions all the time, but never of me. I tried to answer them all sweetly enough so as not to give away how much I hated questions.

"Is Birdie your real name, or is it a nickname?"

"Everybody, my whole life, thinks it is a nickname but it isn't. I'm called Birdie. That's my born name."

"I've never met anybody else named Birdie. How wonderful to have a name that nobody else has," the attending nurse said. I thought she was nice, but I still wished she would stop asking questions.

"Has Slick been acting strangely lately? Anything we should know about?"

"No! He's been absolutely fine until tonight. We was playing miniature golf and he almost passed out. I thought it was just because it was so hot outside. He hasn't been right since then."

"Why didn't you take him to the hospital right away? The sooner that stroke victims can get treatment the better their chances of recovery."

I could feel what was growing: they were trying to blame me for not taking care of Slick when I should, for not understanding. I could see it all amassing in front of me; I was to be blamed.

"How bad is he?"

"We'll have to wait for the doctor to answer that. Is Slick a heavy drinker?"

"No! He never touches a drop!"

"And smoking or chewing tobacco?"

I didn't think the woman was nice anymore.

"Absolutely not! I do not like these questions," I said, apologizing with my tone.

"I'm sorry, ma'am, but we want to help him as much as we can."

"Going home is what would help him. People die in hospitals, not at home where they are safe."

"I assure you, ma'am, they die in both places. Did Slick get a lot of exercise?"

"My lands, yes! He was on his feet all day at the station."

"Yes, but was he physically active otherwise?"

"You mean like taking long walks and things like that?"

"Yes, activities that would have raised his heart rate, like climbing stairs or hills, riding bikes, things like that," the woman said.

"Oh. No. He was too weak for that. He would've just dropped over dead if he'd had to climb a hill. We went to Spring Mill a few years ago and tried to take one of those walks, and those hills just about killed us both!"

CHAPTER 92

I could see it more clearly now. Repetition. I had run up and down hills all my life, and I walked everywhere in the old days—I even walked from Ophelia all the way to other towns if the weather was nice. But since the war and since Slick worked so hard at the station, our leisure time never included a walk. Not once did we ever take a walk in a park, though we drove by many on our way to Sunday shopping trips in Louisville, Evansville, or Bloomington. Why, I wondered, didn't we walk all over the campus of Indiana University, since we drove by it a million times? Oh, how I wanted him to get better so we could do that. Spring Mill again, too, or McCormick's Creek. There was animals there that scared me, but they weren't as bad as the terrible men. I could see them sometimes, even now, when my eyes are closed and I'm waiting on sleep.

In those days after Slick's stroke, all kinds of doctors and nurses came to talk to me. I would not leave his side. I could hardly keep them all straight in my head. They kept saying that his stroke was "minor," but it didn't feel very minor to me. He couldn't walk or talk. They kept saying he had to do his physical therapy. The day he got to the hospital they tried to make him get up and walk! That man couldn't walk, and you could see him struggling. A speech therapist came in and starting making him do exercises with his jaw and his tongue, and all Slick could do was cry from the frustration of it. They were putting this poor man through hell and he was already there!

He was in the hospital for more than a week, and when they let us leave they handed me a stack of papers you wouldn't believe. The biggest thing, they told me so many times, was that physical therapists would come to the house for the next three months, and "This is a crucial time for his recovery."

I'd known of several stroke victims back through the years in Ophelia, and every single one of them recovered by total rest. When I used to pick up injured birds when I was a little girl, they didn't learn to fly again by therapy, did they? I would confine them to a box, feed them, and let them rest. God knows how to heal people if we leave them alone. Those therapists came to the house, one of them a lady, and she talked a blue streak. "Use it or lose it!" she kept saying, as she'd stretch Slick's legs out and make him lift weights with his ankles. She was hurting him and I didn't mind telling her so.

"Birdie, you have to understand that any physical therapy causes pain. It is a cycle of pain and recovery. He can absolutely walk again. I've done this many times. You've got to believe me."

And she went on and on. But there was no way she was going to convince me that she was helping him. I would only let her go so far with him before I told her not to come back. And you know what she said? "If you don't allow me to come back, I will report you to the hospital." Imagine, reporting me! I could see what they were all going to try to say, that I was abusing or something. I was protecting him! They were the ones hurting him. I insisted they show him the same tenderness I'd always showed the birds. I let them come for a few more weeks, just so they wouldn't report me, and they wrote their reports and social workers kept coming to the house, never leaving us alone, trying to convince me to put Slick into a nursing home.

"Even if he spent just a month in a nursing facility, you would see a huge difference when he came home."

I could not imagine Slick spending the night in one of those awful places. It was a mercy to me that Mama never had to do that. She just didn't wake up one morning, at home in her own bed, and that is how Slick would spend his last years, too, I knew that. I was never going to let him waste away in one of those homes. I owed Slick everything, my whole life, so I wasn't about to abandon him when he needed me the most.

CHAPTER 93

Jenny told me very early on that she wanted to work in classical music and opera, and I pooh-poohed that whole idea. I realize I was wrong to do that. Once I realized she was dead serious, I started to turn my words around, as I knew my words were going to be important. It scared me to think of Jenny studying and working a field I knew nothing about and it scared me because I knew it would separate us. I would never be able to travel to where they put on opera, and I would feel so out of place and so stupid that I wouldn't go, anyway. That's the thing with all of the kids: you have to make a world for them that allows them to leave you and that is just so hard. It means you have to say good-bye to them for years and years, not just once but thousands of times.

I wanted Jenny to learn to play the piano so she could be like the ladies I grew up with who could play the spots off anything. Doris was one; she played at the movie house, and she could follow along any movie and play any kind of music in the old silent days. In some ways they were the best movies because they played with your imagination. You had to think about how the actors on the screen might sound if you could hear them. It made me feel like one of the birds, and how the human world must sound to them. They must know we are saying something, but they have to translate it into something they can understand.

Children are interested in everything, though, so it took me some time to figure out just how serious Jenny was about her music. Whenever an opera singer came on *The Tonight Show*, that's usually when I fled to the kitchen, but that's when she became a different child. What I thought were just screamy voices she would hear as incredibly beautiful. There was a big fat singer on there one time, sang some Stephen Foster song with a harp, and Jenny sat on the floor of our living room and cried as she listened to it. She wasn't very old when she said that singing changed her life, even though she would never sing herself. She made me realize, again, that just because you don't hear something doesn't mean it isn't there. Birds hear everything, and nobody wants to admit that they might understand, but I know for certain that they can and they do. They talk about us all the time. This is something I've always known down deep somewhere but never completely understood until that awful night when Stevie hit me and when Ginger got hit by the car and I tasted her blood.

I started buying Jenny records she would ask for, and that embarrassed me to death, too, because I would have to go into some of them shops in Bloomington or Indianapolis and try to not mess up the name of Beethoven, or remember the difference between Schumann and Schubert or Verdi and Wagner, and they were all so hard for me to pronounce. I will say that everybody in those shops helped me because they knew I was a fish out of water, trying to buy old French operas that sometimes even the shopkeepers hadn't heard of.

It felt to me like Jenny hardly had any teenage years, because that Sister Sheila worked her so hard on the piano and she started talking about all kinds of operas. I never even knew that people studied opera that hard. How much could there be to know? Well, Jenny studied all the time. When she came over for her Friday nights with us, she wasn't interested in watching any of the TV shows or doing any of the fun things we did before my forever day. She would sit somewhere in the house and read about French operas, can you beat that?

CHAPTER 94

Opera just sounds wrong to me. False and snooty. But little Jenny wasn't false or snooty. She started studying the oldest operas people could find, and it wasn't long before she knew more about it than her teachers. It all went so fast. In what felt like half a minute to me, Jenny was speaking French and Sister Sheila was taking her to a special library in Bloomington where she could look at really old music from France.

I had a bad feeling about Sister Sheila. It wasn't just that she was taking Jenny away and filling her head with things that I'd never have in mine. It was that Sister Sheila seemed to take over everything. She wasn't a nun like Slick's sister, sweet and insistent. She was a nun who was more like a man. They all got so relaxed about wearing habits, or not wearing them, and Sister Sheila even started wearing pants, which is a step too far if you ask me. Jenny dressed like a little girl until she started piano lessons with that Sister Sheila and then she started wearing pants, and asking for pants for birthdays and Christmas. Sister Sheila made Jenny stop being a little girl, and I just think that is awful. Jenny's parents took a light view of it all. They said Sister Sheila was just "bringing out Jenny's nature" and "helping her discover her passion," and all that nonsense. Nature and passion are dangerous things, and we build houses and shelters to keep ourselves safe from them, don't we?

CHAPTER 95

I realize now that after my forever day, I started to mourn little Jenny as though she had died, even though really and truly, from her point of view, she was just at that moment coming to life. I reckon I couldn't stand the idea that Sister Sheila might have helped her more than I did. I just tried to give all the kids a place where they could be free and act like kids. And if I really told the truth to myself, which they keep trying to tell me to do here, I know that I just wanted to stay a little girl myself, and tending to all the nieces and nephews was the easiest way to do that. All my collectibles—the dolls, the magazines, the salt and pepper shakers—they were just to keep childhood alive for as long as I could, and help me accept that my childhood got stolen from me and nobody really noticed. That awful day all those years ago was a forever day, too, and one that I would have done anything on earth to forget. But since I couldn't forget it, I made all kinds of diversions for myself that would at least keep it on the sidelines. But then life delivers this funny thing to you at the end: it makes sure you don't forget. The forever days, the ones that happen every fourteen years, replay over and over and over and over, until you finally have to do something with what they are saying to you.

CHAPTER 96

People think that your older years move fast, but mine never felt that way. Once Slick had his stroke after my forever day, the time seemed to slow down like one of them glaciers. Suddenly there were generations of birds around the house who I'd never met, and I started to neglect the bird feeders and the sometimes the birdbaths went dry for days and days. I hated that. But once Slick came home from the hospital, there was no letup. The hospital talked a good game to me about how Slick might recover. But it was all talk. The therapists, as they called them, came for months after his stroke, but not a single one of them would listen to me, and I was the only person on earth who really knew Slick.

From that last forever to day to now—well, I don't know how long that has been. I can't imagine that Slick will be able to live much longer. Every once in a while a social worker from the county will come to visit us, and they always try to get me to let Slick be taken to a nursing home, saying he needs "round-the-clock care." Well, what the hell do they think I'm giving him? I only leave the house to go to the drug store and grocery store, and I always try to be sure that Slick is fast asleep during those times so he won't get worried that I'm not there. He frets over the smallest things, and if I'm there to smile at him, it eases his worries. I can't believe how expensive adult diapers are! And he sure went through them. I'd never learned how to change a baby's diaper, not really. But I sure had to learn how to change Slick's. And every single time I had to do it, he would cry, poor thing, embarrassed that anybody had to see him that way. I kept telling him, "I said for better or worse, honey!" I couldn't imagine having some stranger do it every day at a nursing home.

An old priest I'd never seen before came to visit one afternoon. I'd lost all track of time by that point so I couldn't even tell you what year it might have been, but it was shortly before Slick died so I think ten years might have passed since my forever day. I'd been changing Slick's diapers through it all.

The priest sat down and Slick started to cry. Well, Slick cried at the slightest thing as he got older. I was so mad at that hospital for giving me hope that Slick might improve, that his stroke had been "minor," that speech therapy and physical therapy would allow him to return to some kind of "quality of life." But them therapists did not know what they were doing. They were hurting him and I was not going to allow that. So Slick sat in his easy chair, watched television, and cried. I fed him all his favorite foods, and cleaned up when it all came out the other end. That became my life. Then along came this priest.

Even through the stroke, when he couldn't get words out, I could tell what Slick was thinking, and Slick knew this priest, probably for a long time. Slick kept crying and almost laughing, and the priest kept comforting him, gently, like a child.

I finally had to ask. "How do you know Slick, Father?"

"I'm sorry, Birdie. I should have introduced myself, but I assumed you knew. Slick and I knew each other up at Camp McCoy during the war. I was an army chaplain after I shipped out. I brought you back your cuckoo clock."

"You are the cuckoo priest?" I realized how it sounded and winced.

"Yes, ma'am. I'm the cuckoo priest. That wouldn't be the first time I've been called that, I'm afraid. How are you doing during this long ordeal?"

"You mean Slick's stroke? That hasn't been an ordeal. We've had some of our very best times together here at the house. I've enjoyed taking care of him, Father."

"Well, the Lord will bless you for all of your selfless care."

I didn't rightly know what he meant by that.

"Slick and I have known each other for so long and I knew something was wrong because he stopped coming down to St. Meinrad where I live."

"Slick came down to visit you?"

"He came down to hear the monks sing matins and sometimes I would see him, yes. He had to get that station open, as you know."

"Yes. How often would he drive down there and hear the monks?"

"Oh, often. He was a regular at St. Meinrad. Everyone loved seeing him."

"I see." Nothing made any sense to me. I got so muddled with the time and space of what he was telling me. Slick had been in his chair for ten years and I'd never seen this priest before.

I thought of what Stevie had screamed at me that night when he was so drunk.

Stevie was such a help with Slick. He helped me get him to the bathroom and onto the bed so we could clean him and change his diaper. And Slick liked seeing Stevie. He never knew, of course, that Stevie had hit me, and that boy had tried everything he could to put his life back together. He loved playing his music and he got a few "gigs," which I guess just meant jobs, playing weddings and things like that. He didn't make much money, but he didn't need much. He still had all of his equipment out in the garage, and he put a bed and couch out there so he could live in the place. I was happy to have him around for help and running errands. He put a little heater/air conditioner next to where we used to have Ginger's dog pen. When she was a young dog, we would leave her out there when we went on shopping trips or drives, but then I heard about somebody in Ophelia getting their dog stolen, so I never left her out there again. We never got rid of the dog pen, though, and Stevie was so clever about using it to make the garage more livable. His worthless parents never came around to visit Slick. Gerry even said to me that it just "broke her heart" to see him that way, as if she had a heart.

But I was scared to death that Stevie might come in and find that priest with Slick, because I knew how Stevie felt about priests. Even though he'd grown up a lot, he could still be awfully unpredictable.

The priest took Slick's hands. "Slick, I have to tell you something. I'm retiring from the priesthood and the diocese is sending me to New Mexico, where I'm going to spend the rest of my days praying and contemplating. So I won't be seeing you again."

I didn't think much of this, since this priest hadn't seen Slick for the last ten years, anyway, but the news hit Slick like a ton of bricks. He started to sob.

"No! No! No! No leave now!" Slick said as clear as a bell. He had not spoken that many words altogether in months.

"I will be okay. You will be okay. We have a lifetime of memories to keep with us. Never forget that."

"No memory. No memory. Just. Now." I couldn't believe Slick was talking so much.

"It is the church's will that I leave here. So I take that as God's will. I will go to New Mexico and spend the rest of my days praying and asking for absolution of my sins, which have been many."

"No sin. No. Please. No. Leave. Stay." Slick cried and cried.

The cuckoo priest looked at me. "Birdie, would you like me to give Slick the rites of extreme unction?"

"That's for when he is dying. He is not dying," I said.

"It is a Catholic rite for the sick. We believe it will help connect him to the Passion of Our Savior, for whenever he arrives on the other side for his eternal rest."

"Slick hasn't been to church in years, Father," I said, not wanting to refuse the man.

"Slick has remained a faithful Catholic even in sickness, I am certain of it."

Well, I thought, what harm could it do him? It was just some oil. So I agreed.

I never did get his name, and I never could remember the names of priests and nuns. I have no idea how Catholics told them all apart. The priest took a vial of oil from his pocket and spread a little bit of it over Slick's forehead.

The cuckoo clock sounded.

"Through this holy anointing with oil, may the Lord in his love and mercy help you with the grace of the Holy Spirit."

Then he put some oil on the top of Slick's hands and said, "May the Lord who frees you from sin save you and raise you up."

I hadn't expected to hear those words and I blurted, "Stop it! Stop saying those words. Words create things, don't you understand? And if you say those words, you are going to kill him."

"Birdie, do you want Slick to receive the grace of God when he dies?"

"Of course I do, but what I really want is for him *not* to die."

"Well, you know that is impossible, don't you? We all die."

"But not yet. Words kill, I tell you."

"I wish you both peace. I have to go now, Slick."

"No. Go. No. Leave. Stay. Me…"

"I will never forget you, Slick. Thank you. Think of me whenever the cuckoo clock sounds. I've loved hearing it again myself. I can't believe you've kept it working for this long."

And he walked out. Slick was sobbing as I had never seen him sob. And I knew I had no way of really finding out what had gone on between this priest and Slick. I knew something big had happened but I didn't know what.

Slick was never the same after that priest visited. The local priests had come all the time and there had always been polite chats and prayers, but nothing like this. The whole thing feels so foggy to me now that some time has passed. The days run together.

CHAPTER 97

I've been obsessed with death my whole life, from when we had to say good-bye to Daddy so long ago, but real death has nothing to do with what we call death. Real death is letting go of our forever days, isn't it? Those days have to die; we can't just stay in them forever. I'm not good at secrets, though, so I wish they would tell me what comes next. I've been much bolder than I thought I could be in asking them, and they keep saying that whatever comes next is up to me, as though I've ever had any say whatsoever in what happened to me. Too much of my life has been at the mercy of a few men, but I reckon I will figure it out.

I sure worried about Jenny enough for her to be a daughter. Looking back on my forever day now, I realize that I spent more time and attention on Stevie because he needed it the most, but it was Jenny who took more of my thoughts because she just was not like the other kids. I knew how hard it was to have something about you that set you apart. Jenny always knew so much but she wasn't the absolute best at her studies, if you listened to her teachers. I knew early on what her parents wouldn't even think about. I'm not sure how I knew, but as usual, I did, and I know the birds helped me. She found the best kinds of ways to distract herself from all her differences from the other kids, and I still love that about her. She knows more than five other people put together. She just loves knowing things.

CHAPTER 98

It is odd to me about this place, that my forever day doesn't include all of the family. My memories are complete, of course, but a great many of them seem filed away somewhere, not forgotten but not of use anymore. I seem to have some that still need to have something done with them. I have held onto so many memories in my life that it feels odd now to set some of them free.

Jenny wrote all of the time, and those letters kept me going. Before long, the letters were coming from Paris, France! Can you imagine? That little girl who had told me she would someday live in London had landed herself in Paris. From what I could take away from her letters, she went to music school in Paris and they liked her so much that she stayed there. She was always such a funny kid. But she was also going to achieve whatever she wanted. She seems to be studying old French music of some kind. I don't rightly understand it.

I'm terrified now of the Last Judgment. Jenny said in one of her letters that Galileo "had moved the sun from where it had always been," and as I read this I became filled with regret and fear. I'd gone my whole life never knowing even a fraction of what my niece had learned in a just a quarter century.

Learning never bothered me much until I got closer to the end, then I was overtook with the idea that there might be important things for me to know, like Galileo moving the sun. I mean, who moves the sun? How did he do that? I don't even know when Galileo lived. How important is it for us to know things?

I've known a lot about the birds, things that others never knew, things that I could have taught people about. I could have taught it to Jenny, but I was too scared, and now she's in Paris.

I knew there would be some kind of reckoning sometime, but I didn't change my life because of it. I did the best I could. I didn't think it would be like this. Not this.

They are trying to tell me things I just cannot hear. My forever day was over for good from that night Slick passed. Something in me thought I should call an ambulance, but I knew he was going to cross over and I so wanted him to be at home. I didn't get to say good-bye to Mama and I was darned sure I wanted to be there for him.

The reason I could not let go of my forever day is that Slick hurt me so much that night. I know he wasn't all there but still, the words came out of him and they sounded like him. It was him, somewhere in there. He was already in some other place.

"Birdie-wordy, you should have let me die that night we played putt-putt. I've been such a burden to you all these years."

"No! No! No! Slick, you shouldn't ought to say those things. I have loved every minute of these years with you!"

"I can't die without telling you the truth. I wasn't true to you, Birdie. I'm so sorry."

"Honey, you aren't yourself. Don't spend these last minutes worrying about things that don't matter."

"This matters, honey."

"Why? I wasn't able to be a full wife to you. I know that. I understand if you had to go looking. I just don't want to know about it. Please, just don't tell me."

"I confessed it to a priest, but that doesn't seem to make me feel better," Slick said to me, trying to go further.

"Slick, please stop. I can't live with this for the rest of my life! I don't need to know."

"But I need to tell," Slick said. He hadn't put ten thoughts together for years, and suddenly he felt he had to tell me something.

"I drove to St. Meinrad all those early mornings, I really did," Slick said, crying.

"What are you telling me, Slick?" I was crying too by then.

"You've got to tell Father Joe about me passing over. He can't just read it in a church bulletin." Slick cried more.

"What is his name?"

"Father Joe. Everybody at St. Meinrad knows him. He's been there for years."

"Did you go down there to confess and talk to him?" I asked, knowing it was more than that. I got up real close to him because his voice was getting weaker.

"Oh Birdie. I don't know how I'll ever explain it to my maker. It was more. Oh Birdie, I can't face what I've done. Years and years and years. I do love you, my Birdie, and I'm so sorry."

And within a minute, he was gone. Did he really say those things to me? I don't know anymore. All our years together, all our memories, all my taking care of him for nearly ten years as though he was a child, all gone. From that moment I had to live with such a memory. All those boys at the station I saw from the Arrow. All of my years of trying to give myself to Slick but never being able to get there. And more than all of that, I had to say good-bye to him. I had to call the undertaker to come and get him, and call his brothers. It all changed in an instant. They took him out of the house and I was as completely alone as I'd ever felt since the Pinnacle.

CHAPTER 99

After Slick died it felt like I was always walking on sand. He had been my whole purpose in life from the day I met him in 1925, and we were married longer than some people get to live, fifty-nine years. Visitors came and brought all kinds of food. It was nice to see the nieces and nephews again, since I hadn't seen so many of them for ages. Stevie drove me to the funeral parlor to pick out Slick's casket. I nearly fainted when they took me into that room. My sisters had picked out Mama's casket because I was so upset I couldn't get out of bed. I almost had Stevie do it by himself, since I wasn't sure I'd be able to do it. I had been able to shelter myself away from so much in life, and I know death is something we all have to deal with, but the truth is I just don't understand it. I don't understand why anybody has to die, except I guess there would be too many of us if we all stayed around.

But I wanted Mama and Slick to live. We didn't ask much of the world. We didn't take a lot of money from it. We didn't live on a very big property compared to most people. We just had our little corner of Ophelia where we was so happy for a while, just doing normal things: shopping, eating out in all the fun places that sprung up after the war, playing putt-putt golf, walking a dog feeding the birds, and sitting outside on spring nights before the mosquitoes came. That's all I ever wanted out of life. I didn't ask to hear the language of birds. I didn't ask for what happened to me at the Pinnacle all those years ago. I didn't ask for Slick to have a stroke. I didn't ask to just about break my back trying to lift his legs up so I could change his diaper and wash his bottom like a baby. I didn't ask for any of that. All I asked was that something, anything, just stayed itself for a little longer. I just wanted more of what I wanted more of.

And suddenly there I was in a room full of caskets, most of which cost more than our house. I couldn't afford them. The funeral people talked to me about leakage and moisture, things I didn't understand, and Stevie whispered to me that they were trying to get me to spend more by playing on my emotions about Slick's body decaying. I know the way of things, and I knew Slick wasn't in his body now, but of course I wanted to keep his body dry. I couldn't stand to think about putting Slick in the ground at all, much less about thinking of him down there when it rained. I'd buried Ginger in the ground myself, but this was my husband. There was some Bible verse about worms destroying the body. I kept thinking of it even though I didn't want to think of it. Birds eat worms. I couldn't have worms eating Slick. I had to have the casket that kept everything out, so that at some future time if I, or anyone else, ever wanted to see Slick's body again, he would look exactly the same as he did that day. Could they make me sure of that? Yes, they did. Stevie was such a help to me that day. We picked out the casket Slick would be buried in.

And I knew it was something I couldn't talk about later, since people never want to talk about the things that happen after a person dies.

What I hated the most was when people would try to say it was better that Slick died, that he'd "gone to a better place," as though I hadn't been good enough to him.

I don't know how she got there so fast from Terre Haute, but when we got home from the funeral parlor, the nun was already there.

She said what I expected her to say: "He's in a better place now."

That launched me into crying. "I want him here with me, even if you are right."

"I know you do, Birdie. But he is receiving the salvation of the Lord now. And he isn't in pain anymore. He can walk and run and he's with his parents and all of his friends who have gone before him. He is wondering why we are crying. He knows a truth now that was never available before."

"I want to believe you but I just can't, Sister. You don't understand what I've lost."

"Birdie, I've lost my brother."

Well, that jolted me. I hadn't thought about her loss. "I'm so sorry, Sister."

"You will someday be reunited with Slick and your mother and father, and everyone else you've loved. I promise you."

"Pearly gates and all?"

"I think it might just look like something you find beautiful already. If that means pearly gates, then your gates will be the pearliest there are."

I couldn't do anything but cry and hug her.

"Have you spoken to the priest about the funeral service, Birdie? What readings you might like that would be especially meaningful to you? And pallbearers? And music?"

"I need to call Jenny to see if she is coming home from Paris. She could play something, I guess. I don't know anything about readings. Surely some of the nephews would carry him. I can't think."

"I'll take care of all of that. Why don't you rest?"

That's what nuns do. They take care of everything quietly and without any fuss. I didn't have the first idea what to do about anything. I did not know what readings I wanted. Lord almighty! How would I have known that? Heck, we didn't even have a cemetery plot, which I had never once thought about until the nun mentioned it. I always assumed we'd be buried together in the big cemetery on the hill by Mama, but the nun said she would arrange to get us plots in the Catholic cemetery.

I walked through the funeral like I was dead myself. I didn't cry at the church or at the cemetery because I couldn't cry in front of all of them people. I saw so many who used to come around the station all the time, and it was a comfort. But there were also a lot of strangers, people Slick knew but I didn't, and that made me so sad, because I realized there had been parts of his life I never knew about and now never could.

CHAPTER 100

I was afraid the funeral might live in me like a forever day, afraid I might always see Slick lying in his coffin, but that wasn't how it turned out. People came to visit me pretty regular in the weeks after Slick died, and they helped me clear out all the medical things that were all over the house. I nearly collapsed when a nurse came and asked if I would be willing to give my packages of adult diapers to the nursing home. I told her to take them, of course, but as she took big boxes of them out of the basement and loaded them into her car, it made me so sad, which surprised me. They was just diapers, and I didn't need them anymore, but it was hard to let go of them. It felt like I was saying good-bye to a child and in a way I was, because Slick was like a baby for the last ten years of life. Ten years. I couldn't conceive of it being that long.

After a few weeks, though, not many people came by, and I sat alone in the house day after day. Stevie still lived out in the garage but many days I didn't see him at all. I never went out there to check on him, because I always remembered that night when he hit me. I knew he would never hit me again but I lost the energy to go out there. Sometimes I would drive down to the grocery, but I didn't like to because I couldn't bear to let anybody see me. The nieces and nephews usually brought me candies and things when they would visit, and I didn't have much appetite, anyway. A few months after Slick died, I noticed that I sometimes forgot to eat. Suddenly the *Tonight Show* would be on and I would remember, so I'd usually just go to bed.

I did start the bird feeders back up and I was able to buy enough bird seed to keep them all stocked, at least the ones from the windows. I didn't take care of the birdbath anymore, but I noticed Stevie out there sometimes filling it, which always made me happy. My power with the birds was changing, getting weaker and weaker, ever since my forever day. I knew while Slick was sick that I had neglected them and I was trying to make up for it. At first I thought the birds had changed, but as winter came I realized it was me. I was changing. I started to have social workers from the county knocking at my door and bringing me meals from the Senior Citizens Center in Ophelia. They tried like everything to get me to go over to the center for lunch and to play cards, but I was not going to get dressed and go out every day. I didn't see how that was going to make me any better. Slick was dead and there wasn't a darn thing they could do about that. I was grateful that they brought me food because there were many days it was all I had. But some of them social workers were so insistent. They said they'd drive me over to the center for lunch; "You might see somebody you know, or you could meet some new people," they would say to me.

I lost all track of time, so I'm not sure when it was, maybe three years after Slick died, that one of them came and said I had to go to the doctor with her or she would call an ambulance. I would have been embarrassed to death to have an ambulance pull up to my house. I fought all I could to keep from going to the doctor, but I finally had to admit to the hard truth, which was that I could not even walk from the couch to the kitchen anymore, and within a few days I would probably not be able to get up at all. I was absolutely ready to die but that social worker went to Stevie and he came in and told me I had no choice. I had to agree to go to the doctor.

So she took me. I couldn't remember having been at a doctor since I was a little girl. I sure had not seen one since during the war, which that young doctor in Ophelia could simply not believe. I had the social worker with me and he was rough on her. "Why has this woman been allowed to go without medical care for so long? Where have her nieces and nephews been?"

I didn't rightly like that he said those things because it wasn't her fault. And it wasn't the fault of any of nieces and nephews, either. They had all tried for years to get me to go to a doctor, and I just was not about to go. It was my fault.

I'd hardly had anybody ever say things so strong to me as that doctor did. He scared me half to death.

"You are anemic and highly undernourished. I'm not going to allow you to return home. I'm putting you in the hospital for at least a week and then I'll arrange help for you to get into a nursing home. You aren't capable of living alone any longer. I'm very sorry."

I couldn't believe what I was hearing. "But I've just lost my husband. Please don't do this to me."

The doctor didn't even wait. "My understanding is that your husband died nearly three years ago. Is that true?"

"Yes, sir. But it feels like yesterday to me."

"I would be derelict in my duty to allow you to return home. You need to be under medical surveillance for a period of time and then you will need supervision. I'm going to inform the county that you cannot be allowed to live alone."

"But I'm happy at home. Please. I'll go to the hospital and I will eat. I promise."

"I will visit you in the hospital later tonight. You are going to have to have a battery of basic tests, since you have basically been without medical care for decades. I didn't know there was anyone in this county who had not seen a doctor in fifty years."

"I've been just fine until my husband died."

"You have fractures in your back and neck, probably from lifting your husband. There are gynecological issues that need attention. I will find a female doctor for you to talk to about that."

I told him I only wanted one thing. I wanted to go home.

"I'm very sorry, ma'am. I'm not going to send you home to die. My job is to help you live."

"But I'd rather die at home than in a hospital, and I sure can't go to a nursing home."

"Birdie, you are in your nineties. It is okay to need some help." It was the first soft thing he'd said since the social worker made me go see him. Why didn't she just let me stay home and slowly slip away?

CHAPTER 101

Everything after that is still a blur to me. I kept trying to just get back to my forever day. That's the only thing I wanted. All I have are a few flash memories. Once the doctor put me in the Washington hospital, I was so drugged up and so busy that I can't remember any of it. I'd be surprised if I had a drop of blood left after those days. They tested me for everything under the sun. They said I needed iron so they kept making me eat spinach and steak, and I didn't much like either of them. But I did what I was told. They kept trying not to say the words *nursing home* to me, so I heard a lot about *temporary care* and *preventative health*—whatever they were supposed to mean. All I knew was that I was not allowed to go home.

Stevie stayed at my house, in the garage, I guess, but I never knew; and Jenny came to visit at least once that I can remember. I begged her to take me home but she said she couldn't. She would call on the telephone to my room sometimes and I would pretend to talk to her. I loved hearing her voice, but when I wasn't at home I just was never sure what I was really hearing. I would just love the sound of her voice and not really hear anything else. I did love sounds.

The worst part of the nursing home was that it was harder to hear the birds. I could usually convince the nurses to take me to the enclosed patio where I could talk to whatever birds happened to be around, but they weren't my birds. I was just far enough away from home to not be able to call them. I could still see what the birds around me saw, but without enough sound it was just a big blur of lines with pulses, like the machines they had at the hospital. Whatever birds I could see or hear from where I was, I could see and hear whatever they did, which meant I could know a lot about my own surroundings but not much else.

The things about the birds in our yard, if they ever let me go back there, was that I'd spent so much of my life taking care of them; was it so much to ask that they might rescue me now? I was put in that nursing home against my will and I didn't have the energy to fight it. Away from home all I could see was what the birds saw, which meant I couldn't rightly see where I was going and I couldn't figure out why. The birds starting filling my eyes and ears so much that when doctors and nurses tried to talk to me I could barely hear them. It was like they were outside and I was inside trying to hear them through a thunderstorm. I could hear them say things about me and the birds would also report what they was saying once they were out of earshot. There was absolutely nothing that got past me in that nursing home.

I knew several of the people in there from back through the years, but most of them had lost their minds. Mine wasn't gone but it surely wasn't mine anymore, either. The only thing I wanted, every minute of every day, was to get back to my house. Every time Stevie visited, I would beg him to take me home, but he would tell me he couldn't. I asked him once if he was still in the garage and he said yes, but the birds told me he was lying. They said they'd heard he was sleeping in Slick's bed. As long as he wasn't in Mama's room where little Jenny used to sleep, I was okay with it.

They had good food at the nursing home and I ate every bite of everything they ever put in front of me. As I got my strength back, the birds started getting more and more forceful with me, helping me find a way back home. But the nursing home people put a bracelet on my ankle that I couldn't take off, even when they gave me a shower. At first I didn't know what it was for, but I finally found out it was to keep me from running away. If I went through the front door that bracelet would trip an alarm and they would come after me. I was in prison.

I made friends with one little pissant sparrow. Oh my, he was such a scheming little guy. He would sometimes come into the building when the linen truck was doing deliveries and pickups. I always kept a little bread for him in my hand. He got to where he would come right onto the arm of my wheelchair without any fear at all. He didn't make much noise, as sparrows usually don't, so the nurses didn't seem to notice him.

I called him Clem because he reminded me of a guy named Clement who was a friend of Daddy's. Clem would sit with me for long periods, and he told me some of the most amazing things. I hadn't had the heart to look in a mirror in ages, but I could see myself through the sparrow's eyes. He saw me as I used to be. Young and ready for an adventure, the way I used to run around House Rock and the Pinnacle and go over to Hindostan and swim. He saw all of that when he saw me. I just loved that little guy. He even got down on the ground and pecked away at the little bracelet on my foot.

The linen truck came once a week, and they left the side door to the center wide open the whole time no matter what the weather. My days might have run together but I sure remember the day the nurse gave me my bath and didn't put on my alert bracelet. She said it had gotten damaged somehow and she would get me a new one, but she forgot to do it. Next thing I knew, Clem was guiding me toward the linen truck and it was no trouble at all to climb up in the back of it, because they had steps and all, and find a corner to hide in. That gorgeous little Clem even joined me in the truck. The people carrying the linens in and out of the center never saw me. I knew little Clem would help me once we got to wherever we were going.

I had so many days at the center when they'd make me talk even though the only thing I wanted was to be quiet and listen to the birds. In that truck piled floor to ceiling with linens, I was in the quietest place I'd been for years. I could have rode around in that truck for hours, but it didn't take us long before I heard the door open. As soon as I could, I peeked around the corner to see if I knew where we were. Sure enough I didn't, but Clem did. He gave me the all clear and I got right out of there. I must have looked a sight just wearing my housedress but I was so happy to be free that I didn't care. They'd stopped at one of the big fancy houses near the Pinnacle, can you imagine? I was exactly where I wanted to be. I hadn't had that much energy in years. I headed down the hill to Jug Rock and all the way down to House Rock without anybody noticing. Clem took off into the woods after he was sure I had escaped. There it was, towering over me in the cool of autumn: the Pinnacle.

CHAPTER 102

I didn't know where I was when I woke up. They gave me a paper by accident, but I still don't know what it meant. "Subject has hypertrophic accumulation of childhood emotions, and is mired in a series of traumas she lacks the cognitive powers to assess and discard."

I heard a man talk to a lady in the room. "Are you her niece? Sorry, she wasn't supposed to see that." I would have sworn he was talking to Jenny.

"Yes, I've just flown in from Paris, so I don't know exactly what time zone I'm in. Sorry." It sure enough sounded like her.

"Your aunt is being kept alive with potassium at this point. She refuses to eat. There was some hypothermia from her exposure several days ago, but that seems to be slowly healing."

"Does she talk?" Jenny asked.

"Oh yes, quite a lot. She is perhaps having delusions. We can't, of course, be sure," the doctor said.

"How much longer does she have?" Jenny asked. I knew I wasn't supposed to hear them so I pretended to be asleep.

"It is difficult to say. She is almost a hundred years old from what I understand. She wasn't very happy with telling us her age. Or anything else, for that matter." The doctor laughed.

"Yes, she is in her late nineties. Her husband has been dead for ten years. She was doing okay for a while. I called a lot and visited when I could. Sent money. But over the past few years, it has been very difficult for her. Lots of loneliness. And the younger members of the family don't visit like we all used to. She was like a mother to me."

"Well, I would imagine that we are talking about a matter of hours now, not days. It is great that you are here, and you should spend whatever time she has left together, if you can," the doctor said. He sounded polite so I knew he wasn't that awful doctor who put me away.

"Aunt Birdie, can you hear me?" Jenny said.

"My lands! What a sight, honey!" I said, weakly.

"Direct from Paris, France! It's just like the slides you used to show me." Jenny laughed.

"Where the hell do you buy groceries?"

"You remembered!"

"I remember everything. They think I'm in here wasting away and I can see that my body is on its last legs. But not my memories." I surprised myself with how much energy I had. "What year is it?"

"It is 1998, Aunt Birdie."

"I can't hardly believe that. You are living in Paris. Have you been to a movie lately?"

"The big movie right now is about the *Titanic*."

"Lordy, I was alive for the play, not the movie! I saved every magazine and newspaper from those weeks. They are all downstairs. You have to promise me to save them."

"Yes, of course, Aunt Birdie. How are you feeling?"

"I feel tired."

"You have to eat, you know. The doctors say you won't eat," Jenny said.

"I don't have much appetite, to tell you the truth."

"Would you eat if I ate something with you?"

"Well, I just might," I said.

Jenny had the nurses bring in a tray of food. Having flown directly from Paris she was hungry herself, so she took a bread roll off my tray and bit into it. I was glad she did. She started feeding me and was surprised when I ate, slowly at first, then everything else on the tray. Jenny sent for more. I ate that, too.

"I've already been to Paris, you know? Ever since Slick died I could go anywhere I wanted," I said.

"You came to Paris and didn't come calling? That's not very nice." Jenny laughed.

"Stevie has been to visit. He's such a good boy," I said.

"I thought Stevie had moved out of Ophelia to somewhere out west."

"Yes, of course. You're right," I said. I feel half-cuckoo these days. "I have all those photo albums for you. They should go to the youngest in the family."

"Hedy's children are the youngest in the family, Aunt Birdie," Jenny gently said.

"Bleedin' Jesus, you don't think I'm going to let her get her mitts on my photo albums! She's a thief!" I said to her strongly. "Are you still about to turn into a hamburger?"

"I'm a vegetarian now, can you believe it?"

I told her, "I want you to be sure that all my favorite salt and pepper shakers are given away to nieces and nephews. But you take the best ones for yourself, now."

"Do you still have the cuckoo clock?"

"Well, I don't rightly know what is at the house. I haven't been there in the longest time. A priest bought that clock for Slick during the war. Oh, that is so long ago now."

Jenny said she would go over to the house at some point and check on everything for me.

CHAPTER 103

It was such a joy that I thought it might become another forever day. We talked through the night, all about the old days, Jenny's career at the Paris Conservatory. I just couldn't imagine that this was my little niece I'd cared for all those years ago, who learned to play the piano in my house! Jenny tried to explain to me what she did, that she researched and studied old operas—"very old operas," especially the "baroque" operas of France—and she had to explain to me what all of that meant, and I pretended I understood. I thought all operas were old. I couldn't rightly understand why anyone would be interested in *any* opera, old or new, French or otherwise. But I did love that she loved it. Jenny said something to me I didn't understand, but it did stay with me, when I told her how proud I was of her job in Paris. "Being an artist is a philosophy, not a profession, not a hobby, not a job." It might have been a little dig at what I said, with me calling her life in Paris a job, but I reckon she deserved it after saying that "most people's idea of a great pianist is Liberace" years ago.

"Aunt Birdie, tomorrow is Sunday. I'm not about to leave on a Sunday. It is just too sad. I'll stick around here for a few days." That made me feel safe.

It came time to tell it, so I started talking to her but I felt like I was outside myself, flying around, and I could hear what I was saying but it was like it wasn't me, more like a movie of me. I think Jenny was there with one of the doctors. I finally told her what had happened that made them take me to the hospital.

CHAPTER 104

It was cold that day so I didn't think there would be snakes around. But we went to House Rock with our lunches and Lucy and I sat down on a sloping part and I thought there was a big crack in the rock. Then I saw it move. I screamed bloody murder and that darn Lucy laughed at me. "That snake is more scared of you than you are of it!"

"The hell it is!" I screamed. I think I could have actually killed my own sister, I was so mad at her. Something had sure scared that big black snake. I threw my lunch all over the place and ran a ways from House Rock, and Lucy just laughed. I was out toward the clearing near the river, and when I stopped to breathe I could hear something. At first I thought it was a boat, and even now all these years later I don't know why I didn't run when I realized it wasn't. I screamed to Lucy that there was bad people coming. I could just feel it. The snake had been the warning, and all the birds around had scattered, trying to tell me to run away. Lucy ran away. I thought of the gypsies. The sound of a train echoed from some strange place I'd never heard before, but the valley was like that. Sounds came from all kinds of places that you knew couldn't be right. Your mind would play tricks with the sounds.

It is so hard for me not to cry. I know what they are doing. For the longest time I thought they wanted me to forget my forever day. But I know I now that I don't have to forget. All I have to do is move. Nothing stops. They wasn't gypsies at all. It was two boys I'd never seen before but they were dressed like rich boys, like they were from the dome. I didn't know what they were up to or why they wanted to be around Ophelia instead of playing with their own kind. It was winter and there weren't no leaves on the trees or bushes to hide behind, and the bare trees changed the sounds, too. I saw them before they saw me. They didn't have guns so they wasn't hunting. I guess they was out for a walk in the woods. Lucy was way out of earshot by then.

I thought I'd die when them boys talked to me. They was older, but still kids. I heard them talking before they saw me. They didn't sound like they came from anywhere around Ophelia. Big-city boys, I was sure.

"We're trying to find the Pinnacle. Do you know where it is?" one of them asked me.

I couldn't speak for a while, but they kept asking me.

"My lands! We are standing right under it. Look up!"

We all laughed and I was so relieved to laugh and not be scared.

I told them that the top of the Pinnacle was the very best place around for a view. "You can see for miles from up there," I told them, and I showed them the path to climb to the top, told them about the House Rock and Jug Rock, things they might be interested in.

"What can you see from here, little lady?"

I didn't like the way he asked me that, but I answered him, anyway: "You can see the river, and the Pinnacle looks beautiful from down here, rising above you like a great cathedral." I'd remembered Mama saying that at some point. I would never have thought to call it a cathedral on my own.

"I know I speak for my friend here when I say we don't rightly take much interest in a cathedral," one boy said.

I'd been scared a lot in my life but this was the first time I'd felt real terror. I knew they were going to hurt me. I've tried so hard for my whole life to forget what happened next that I sometimes wonder if it is real. The doctor people told me the other day that sometimes our memories here are like that, that they won't seem like they are the truth, and we have to learn how to tell the difference. I know what is true. I just haven't been able to move on from it, for what reasons I don't know.

One of the boys grabbed me and put his hand over my mouth to hush me. He pulled me down to the ground. He was so strong there was not a thing I could do. The other boy was laughing, and the more I cried and screamed the more he laughed. I thought they was going to kill me. Mama talked about that type of thing happening sometimes out in the country, but I hadn't paid much mind. They all talked about the gypsies and how they would take little girls, but these boys weren't gypsies. When I try to think about it now, as I know I have to, I wish they had killed me instead of what they did.

The boy who did it to me, if you'd seen him out someplace with his parents, you'd have thought he was handsome and nice. I could smell liquor on both of them, and I'm sure that made them do things they might not have done if they'd been normal. The one boy held me down and told me not to be afraid, that they didn't want to hurt me, they wanted to make me feel good. His voice softened and he felt kindly at first, as the other boy got on top of me. I'm getting scared all over again just remembering it. All these years have gone by and no one knows about it, at least no one who is still around.

It felt like he was tearing into my body with a knife. I screamed so loud that even the boy holding me couldn't muffle it. The boy who was inside me told me to stop screaming and he wouldn't hurt me anymore. He told me to relax and enjoy it because it was going to happen whether I screamed or not. I'll never forget the sound of his voice. "I've got to have some relief, stuck at that boring hotel, so you just keep quiet, little lady." I cried and cried but as hard as I tried, I couldn't get quieter. And I knew what the birds had told me was right: he was from the dome.

It didn't take very long. He moaned and I felt him release something into me, something that felt like vomit gone to the wrong place.

"Jesus, man, she pissed all over the place," the boy said as he stood up and put his pants on. The boy who had been holding me moved me over to a little clearing and turned me over. "It's my turn, little lady. Get on your hands and knees."

I couldn't do it. I was so scared and weak that I couldn't do what he wanted, but he made me do it, anyway. He pushed my face down into a bunch of leaves and everything gets foggy after that. The pain started again, like I was being stabbed. Winter birds were gathering all around. I could hear them. Then I saw the worst thing of all that day, even worse than the boys who were hurting me: crawling toward me through the leaves was a big copperhead snake. I knew right then and there that I would die before I could have a snake crawling on me. It was getting closer and closer and I was feeling faint. So much had happened. When the snake got so close to me that I could see its eyes, a bird swooped down and carried it off. That bird saved me. I'd never seen it before and never saw it again. It was some kind of hawk, and he carried off that copperhead.

Some distance away there was a gunshot and the birds whooshed up and scared us all. The boys ran away back toward town and left me there by myself in the mud and the leaves. Even though I was relieved that they ran away, I couldn't stop crying. Even when I saw who had shot the gun and who had come to find me. It was Daddy. Lucy must have told him that she'd left me in the woods and somebody was there. Maybe he'd heard me crying. I don't know. All I know is there he was. He picked me up and I held him like I'd never ever let go. I couldn't stop crying and screaming while he carried me home. Mama helped me clean up a little bit then Daddy took us both to the train station. Mama was taking me to a doctor in Bedford, about half an hour away by the next train.

CHAPTER 105

Once we were on the train, Mama helped me stop crying. She told me we were going to Bedford to visit a special doctor and I may have to stay there for a few days. I wasn't scared, because it was Mama telling me. Finally I had to tell her for real what happened, so I did. I told her, and I meant it, that I went to the Pinnacle that day because of the leaves that were falling from the trees. They were leading me down all of the paths. I knew the leaves were falling because they were dead and it was their time but I had to follow them. I told her that gypsies had done it to me. I don't know why I told her that, but I remembered her warning me about the gypsies and I guess that's what brought it to my mind.

The doctor was very nice at first, but before long he was asking me questions about what happened to me, and I told him it was gypsies. Mama stayed right in the room with me, right up until he said he'd have to examine me. I screamed as loud as I could possibly scream when he tried to look between my legs, and that is the last thing I can remember from Bedford.

I woke up back in Ophelia at old Miss Maggie's house, and I was so confused that I wasn't home, which was just down the street. Miss Maggie was putting hot and cold compresses on my head and trying to get me to drink water. I called for Mama and she was there in no time; I still don't know how. I asked Mama why I was at Miss Maggie's instead of being at home, and she told me I was just supposed to rest there for a few days. She asked me again if it was gypsies and my head was so foggy that I said I didn't rightly know. I remember Miss Maggie saying, "That's just the ether talking, Beulah, don't you worry about that," or something like that. Mama stayed with me until I fell asleep again. Miss Maggie's house was for midwifing, and I could not for the life of me figure out why I had to stay there.

CHAPTER 106

Now, a lifetime later, they tell me they found my small wounded body near the Pinnacle, right at the spot where the worst thing of my life happened almost ninety years before. Must have been. I have no idea how I got there but I remember them finding me, just like Daddy came to find me when I was a little girl lying in the same spot and he carried me home. But those poor men the other day had to carry me out of there on a gurney. But they weren't the mean men from before.

"Can you tell me how you got here, ma'am?" one of them asked me. He sounded so kind.

"A bird brought me down here. He guided me right down the path, just like the birds always have."

"Can you tell me who you are?"

"I'm Birdie. Everybody here knows me."

"We're taking you to the hospital in Washington. Do you understand that?"

I told him no! And I told him to take me right home but he would not listen to a word I said. I didn't have my pocketbook or anything else that would have told them who I was. And they asked me so many questions it made me dizzy.

"Who is the President?"

"That Bill Clinton, I think."

"That's right. Do you know what year it is, Birdie?"

"Aren't we in the '90s?"

"It is 1998, Birdie. When were you born?"

"It can't be 1998! Where's Mama?"

"Your mother must be dead, Birdie."

"No! I told her it was the gypsies down by the Pinnacle that hurt me. She told me if I was lying I'd have to go to the woodshed."

"Birdie, you don't have to go to the woodshed. You just need to tell us what happened at the Pinnacle. Why were you there, and how did you get down there?"

"It was the gypsies."

"There aren't any gypsies in Indiana, ma'am."

"I'm not lying, Mama. There was gypsies at the Pinnacle and along by House Rock. Can I go to see Doc Mary?"

"Ma'am, you are in an ambulance on the way to the hospital. It is 1998. Your mother is not here."

"I heard Mama say to a doctor we didn't know in Bedford, 'We are from Ophelia, and everyone there would know what happened if I took her to Doc Mary. That's why I brought her up here on the train. I've seen lives ruined by just the rumors, much less the truth. If my little girl was harmed by gypsies, I can't imagine what would happen. There would be posses and hangings; I couldn't bear to be responsible for that. You have to help us.' That doctor was so nice for a while.'"

"Do you want to tell us what happened, Birdie? When was this?"

"I wasn't even ten years old I guess. Lordy, you are going to tell me that is almost ninety years ago and I'm not going to believe you! It was before the first war."

"Go on, ma'am. Tell us."

"All these questions. The doctor in Bedford, that's the other direction, you know...asked me the same thing. He called me 'little Birdie.'"

"What did you tell him, Birdie? Can you remember?"

"My friends and me was all at House Rock, and I heard them a ways away. I was scared but I thought we would all stay there together. But my friends up and left. When the gypsies got there I was so scared that I couldn't run."

"Tell me what happened then." His voice was so gentle and the ambulance was going so fast but I wasn't scared.

"They said they wanted to see the Pinnacle. I couldn't hardly understand them; they said it like the card game Mama plays with her friends. I asked if they wanted to see the top or bottom of it, they said the bottom. I thought that wasn't quite right because everybody wants to see the view of the river from the top of the Pinnacle but I was scared so I took them where they wanted."

"Go on," the doctor said.

"I'm too scared to tell you," I said through the beginnings of tears.

"You can tell me. Why are you embarrassed?"

"I wet myself. I was so scared and I needed to get home and when we got the Pinnacle I just wet myself."

That doctor in Bedford, a kindly man, said, "I'm so sorry, honey. But that's nothing to be ashamed of. You are a little girl and you have to go to the bathroom sometimes. Can I take a look at you, honey?"

I cried so loud when he asked if he could look at me that nurses and doctors all came rushing in to see me. That nice doctor said to Mama, "Miss Beulah, I've not been allowed to examine the girl. I beg you to let us sedate her so that I can."

I couldn't believe it but Mama said he could, and she left. I never felt so alone in my life.

The next thing I could remember was waking up in a small white room with the veins of winter trees outside lightly blowing across the window, and I heard Mama's voice. I asked her where I was.

"You are almost home, little Birdie. We brought you to Miss Maggie's house down the block so you could rest and get better from your examination," Mama said.

I remember asking her, "Why are we at Miss Maggie's house? That's where women come to have babies. What is happening?."

"You are not going to going have a baby, but Miss Maggie was nice enough to let you stay here for a few days while you rest. I'll stay right here by your side," Mama said.

All I could do was cry and beg to go home.

"You will, child. In just a few days. And you won't remember any of this awful time. It will all be lovely again very soon. You'll be playing with your girlfriends and you'll even go down to the House Rock again and play in the woods."

I knew Miss Maggie because she was our neighbor. If I'd been in a different bedroom of her house, I could have seen our place down the road. I didn't like the sounds I was hearing ring through the rafters of her house, but Miss Maggie was the first person I ever saw divine things like the birds do. It was her great gift to sense sadness everywhere and not let it go; she could sit for hours on the walkway of a house when she sensed there was crying going on inside. Not every girl in Miss Maggie's was a mother. Sometimes they just had a feeling of pain from not being mothers. After my long sleep, and I didn't know how long it had been, I became aware of new ways of being aware: sometimes I was myself and I felt all of the fear and sweetness of being a little girl. But at other times, I felt something wetter, something that dilutes everything around, that softens the edges of things. I was me but I wasn't me, like something you wear that don't quite fit.

Out of nowhere, long after the first war, Mama asked me, "Did one of them touch you?"

"Who, Mama?"

"One of them gypsies?" Mama asked gently.

"Yes, ma'am. But I made them stop."

"How did you do that, child?"

"There was huge flocks of birds, Mama." I wanted so to tell her everything but my mind was getting foggy.

"Birdie, we haven't had those big flocks for years; they've all died off. All of those passenger pigeons that used to darken the skies, they're gone. You must be remembering something else. You don't make up, things, child. Tell me how you made them stop."

"The doctor must have told you, so I don't need to."

Mama never asked me again.

CHAPTER 107

There was one nice doctor at the hospital, so I told him, "Mama used to put butter on my burns whenever I was outside too much."

"Have you been burned, ma'am?"

"I don't think so, honey, but my skin feels so hot," I told him Then I noticed that Jenny was there, too, and that made me confused. I don't know why, but I said, "Mama, the birds tried to tell us about the flood."

"Of course, they did, Birdie. You know I'm not your mama; I'm Jenny."

"No, really. They did, and they are trying to tell us something now, Mama. I just can't quite tell what it is."

"Now, Birdie, you know the birds can't talk."

"But you said yourself that if a buzzard's shadow passed over you, it meant you were going to die, but if the shadow of an eagle passed over you it meant you'd get rich."

"Those are just fun old wives' tales, Birdie. Stories. Nothing more."

I reckoned she was right but I loved my stories.

CHAPTER 108

That *Wizard of Oz* was on television and I told Jenny the color wasn't working in the hospital and I could not think about anything else. I told her I remembered that movie being in color. She told me that the whole beginning of the movie was in black and white and then it switches to color when Dorothy gets to Oz, but I didn't remember that at all. I thought she was lying to me and it made me upset. But then the tornado came and sure enough, when she opens the door from her little house into Oz the whole world is in color. How could I have forgotten that? Isn't it funny what you don't remember?

CHAPTER 109

"You remember when we used to drive you around the countryside, honey?" Jenny said to me.

"There was nothing to see," I told her, even though there was everything to see.

"There was everything to see, Aunt Birdie." Jenny laughed.

"I wouldn't let Slick drive over that N.H. Bridge because it was old and rickety and it scared me," I said, and she looked like I'd hit her.

"Now Aunt Birdie, you know that is called Brickyard Road, and we don't call it that awful thing you call it."

"You are the only person on the face of the earth who calls it Brickyard Road. Lordy, we haven't even had a brickyard since the '30s. We all have called it Nigger Hole Bridge for our whole lives. We don't mean anything by it. It is just what we say. Lands, we used to eat Nigger Babies candy and that didn't say anything to anybody!"

"Sometimes you have to make yourself break bad habits, Aunt Birdie. You are talking about a place where there was a lynching. That is not something that needs remembering."

"A lynching? What are you talking about? There never was a lynching in these parts." I'd lived in Ophelia my whole life and I would have known about it. We weren't a place that lynched people.

"I don't want to belabor this, Aunt Birdie."

I didn't rightly know what *belabor* meant but I guessed that it had something to do with talking about it all too much.

Jenny went on, "But the reason you call it 'N-hole' is because two African-American men came through here before World War I and they were suspected of a crime or something, even though it doesn't appear to me from reading the reports that they had done anything. And because of fear and prejudice, they were taken out to the Brickyard Bridge, tied up, weighed down with rocks, and thrown off the bridge into the water. Nobody ever found their bodies and nobody in the town ever talked about it again."

I'd never heard a word about any of that in all my years at the phone office. And when did we start having to call them "African-Americans" instead of "black" or "Negro," or whatever they decided they wanted to be called that year?

"I would have heard about it at some point," I said, sure I was right.

"It was before you worked at the phone office. And there was nothing for you to hear. Nobody ever said a word about it again. But every time you call the place 'N-hole,' you are bringing that memory back to the place and keeping it alive. Do you understand?"

"Well, I can't very well start calling it 'Brickyard Road' at this point in my life. I'd never remember that. I can barely remember the things I'm supposed to remember," I told her, as honest as I could be.

"Well, this all started with you and Uncle Slick driving me around the countryside. I got very interested in everything we saw. Every little hill has a story. I study old things now, all day long, and I think it is because of our drives."

I liked it when she told me about things we did that affected her life. She was such a special girl to me.

CHAPTER 110

I realize now that I slowly built a life I could only describe it as a *nest*, to protect me from anything painful. For years I had visions of a series of closing doors, and I realize now that I was the one closing them, slowly, every day, behind which I left anything painful. Now, over here, I seem to have to open them all again. Nothing can remain closed here. You have to open them all before you can leave.

Slick's church taught that the state of your soul at the time of your death is vital to what happens after, which always ticked me off. I knew what some of the people in town had gotten up to, yet those nuns and priests want us to believe that just because they had God on their lips at the moment of their passing on, it's all fine? I know I'm not the brightest person who has ever lived, but who in their right mind could possibly believe that? It is what you built up, the small kindnesses that you accumulated every day, month by month, that decide what happens to you. I know I have a lot of work to do before I can move on.

CHAPTER 111

We drove to Louisville for two nights for our honeymoon, and I know Slick thought our wedding night would probably go like any other couple's, and we never once talked about it. I was so scared.

Slick hugged me when we got into the hotel room, and I kissed him all over his head and neck, but I had trouble kissing him on the mouth. I don't know why. Slick got a little more forceful and drew me close. "I do love my Birdie-wordy," he said. He was so sweet.

"I love you, too, my darling, and thank you for loving me." Even saying that much made me cry. And I let him kiss me. I could feel his hands all over my back, which felt just wonderful. He started to unbutton my blouse and I stopped him.

"Are you not ready, my sweetheart?" he said.

I started to cry. "I'm not right down there." Oh, even now it makes me afraid to say it.

"What do you mean, Birdie?" He was so polite.

I told him I was hurt down there once and I've never been right since. "Oh, you must hate me!"

"Of course I don't hate you. Do you want to tell me what happened?" Slick was as sweet as I'd thought he was from the first moment I saw him. He never lost that sweetness.

"Oh, no. I can't! I think I'd die if I ever have to talk about that!" I couldn't believe I'd told him as much as I had.

"Are you sure you are hurt? Should you see a doctor?"

I was so embarrassed that I'd never told him any of this before. I knew I should have. "I saw that doctor in Bedford when I was a little girl. He told Mama I was hurt and I couldn't ever have children. She tried to tell me for years and I'd never let her say it. Oh Slick. You won't want to be with me now."

"Of course I want to be with you. You are my Birdie-wordy. But that was years ago. I think you should see a new doctor. They know a lot more now."

"No. I hate doctors. And they will put me on that awful table with stirrups like for a chicken." I tried not to let it sound funny.

Slick was talking stronger now. "They will not hurt you. You need to see someone."

"No. I will give you all the love and attention you will ever want, and I will cook and clean and support everything you do, but I can't give you that. I'm so sorry. I can't. Not ever." It felt like I was slipping through a door that was closing behind me.

"You deserve to know that pleasure, Birdie. We all do."

I knew he was right, but I also knew there was almost no chance I ever would.

"I can't, Slick. I will totally understand if you want to leave me because of it. And I should have told you but I just couldn't figure out a way to say it. I'm so sorry. But I will make it up to you in other ways, I promise."

"You just need to feel less nervous. We can wait."

"No, I'm not nervous. I won't be able to give you that. I can give you everything else, but don't ask me to give you that."

"Let's talk to a doctor together."

"No. No. No."

CHAPTER 112

We did go to bed together for the first time that night, and he held me for a few minutes before he drifted off to sleep. He always could fall asleep anywhere at any time. Years later I walked into the station one night and he was asleep with the cash register wide open—thousands of dollars open to the world!

I lay awake that night and nearly every other night of our lives together for more than an hour, worried about what I'd just told him. I never did sleep very well. I knew I was right to be honest with him but I also worried I'd be alone. I worried about both things at once. I'd let him think all this time that he was going to have a normal marriage. And I guess I'd hoped to myself that by the time the wedding night came around I might be able to get beyond all my horrible shame. I'd hoped I'd be able to let him touch me, but I just couldn't. I didn't have the monthly times that all the women talked about, so I knew I couldn't get pregnant at least. But I should have been able to just have relations, but I was too scared. I knew it would hurt and remind me of that time. Every time I thought about it, my chest tightened and it was hard to breathe. That doctor told me I had a small windpipe, and he used a lot of other fancy words, too, but I knew that whenever something made me feel anxious it felt like my throat was closing and I couldn't swallow and my breath got short. All I could do at those times was try to drink some water or have a little piece of bread, something to make it go away.

Sometimes my short breathing would come in those long hours before I could fall asleep, when I would lie in bed listening to Slick sleep. I thought about my failings every day, and every day I'd hope that Slick would forget it all for one more day, just one more day. I was so grateful he never left me because of it.

CHAPTER 113

"You do my nails when I die, in the color I like, or I'll come back to haunt you," I said to Jenny, not knowing if I would really be able to visit her from the other side.

I felt safe when Jenny told me she was going to stay a few days. Stevie couldn't stand to come to the hospital. I guess it was just too hard for him to see me like that, but other familiars came in to see me. Some of the doctors was really nice. But I most liked having Jenny there with me, and sometimes she played the piano they had down the hall. That made me remember my wonderful forever day when she would play all the hymns and go through all my sheet music.

I remember it so clear now. She told me she had to go back to Paris the next day and she would be saying good-bye.

"Don't say good-bye yet, honey. I love having you here," I said to her.

"I have to go back to work, Aunt Birdie, back to my life in France."

"Will you come back?"

"Of course I'll come back, but will you be here when I come back?" Jenny asked, looking me right in the eye.

I told her I wanted to be.

She said, "You know, Aunt Birdie, it is okay to let go and stop holding on."

I didn't rightly know what to say. I thought it might be one of those times when people talked around things instead of saying exactly what they meant, the way the priests used to do, or whenever I had to talk about the Pinnacle.

"Aunt Birdie, why did you go back to the Pinnacle last week? They found you outside in the cold, and you didn't know where you were. Do you remember that?" Jenny asked me.

"I told Mama that the birds tried to tell us about the flood."

"Of course they did, Aunt Birdie."

"No, really. They did, and they are trying to tell us something now, Mama. I just can't quite tell what it is."

"Now, Aunt Birdie, you know the birds can't talk."

I couldn't quite tell who was speaking, but I answered, "But you said yourself that if a buzzard's shadow passed over you, it meant you were going to die, but if the shadow of an eagle passed over you, it meant you'd get rich."

"Those are just fun old wives' tales. You mustn't pay them any mind."

"Them mean people over the window won't let me leave here." I was surprised by the words coming out of me because I didn't remember ever seeing people over the window. But sure enough, there they were.

Jenny said, "Do you want to leave by the window, Aunt Birdie? It's winter, you know, and very cold."

"I know it is cold now. I've been here since the fall, haven't I?"

"Yes. Was it really gypsies that hurt you, Aunt Birdie? Can you tell me?"

"No, I blamed it on the gypsies because they was who everybody blamed everything on. It was those rich boys from the West Baden Hotel out joyriding. Just a few years later, when Jerry Ballard asked me out, I put two and two together and realized he was one of the boys who hurt me. I've never been able to get over it in my whole life. I guess now I can."

"Yes, Aunt Birdie. It is okay. You can get over it," Jenny said, so kind.

CHAPTER 114

I started seeing more and more. I got frantic. "You have to stop them, don't you understand? It may be two years, five years, I don't know. But the birds have been flying into windows here all day, and they are flying into the walls, too. Why isn't anybody listening? It's not something I'm making up. Oh, I don't know these words. They are telling us that something horrible is growing in the world from horrible, horrible people. Worse than the Japs and the Krauts ever could have been. This is new. They are here in the country. I can hear it and sometimes I can see it. I see what they see when everything is just so. The birds know that they are learning to fly. The radio waves. The signals. Our phone calls. Do we think they can't tell what we're saying? We have to listen to them. Somebody smarter than me has to listen to them!"

Jenny asked me, "If I open the window and ask the mean people to leave, do you think they will?"

"I think they just might," I said, and darned if Jenny didn't walk right over to that window and I heard every word she said.

"Listen here, all of you. I have to go back to Paris tomorrow and my Aunt Birdie says you are being mean and keeping her from leaving. I want you to let her through."

Jenny opened the window and it was cold for a minute. I saw a cardinal. I knew my time was coming because I felt the shadow of a bird pass over me. The Catholics got that one right: cardinals appear when angels are near.

CHAPTER 115

I saw myself lying down in the bed and I looked closely at my own eyes, my nose, my tiny little arms, even my fingernails, up super-close. I was so thin there wasn't much of me left to look at. And very quickly, my forever days were all gone and I was flying. It was cold but I was warm. I wasn't scared anymore, but it also wasn't anything like what they all used to talk about. I flew out over the Pinnacle, past the river, over my house, Mama's house, and all the gravesites, including the one that would soon be my own. I could see the sun to my right and I still had a moment of being me, of understanding, before something else drew me toward it. We migrate north to south using the sun, and some force pulls us there. Maybe I will see a seagull now.

Good-bye.

www.ingramcontent.com/pod-product-compliance
Lightning Source LLC
Chambersburg PA
CBHW020637260626
47157CB00008B/2786